MEET BEHIND MARS

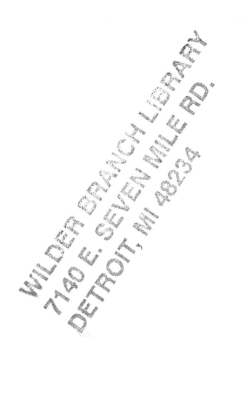

MADE IN MICHIGAN WRITERS SERIES

GENERAL EDITORS
Michael Delp, Interlochen Center for the Arts
M. L. Liebler, Wayne State University

ADVISORY EDITORS
Melba Joyce Boyd
Wayne State University

Stuart Dybek
Western Michigan University

Kathleen Glynn

Jerry Herron
Wayne State University

Laura Kasischke
University of Michigan

Thomas Lynch

Frank Rashid
Marygrove College

Doug Stanton

Keith Taylor
University of Michigan

A complete listing of the books in this series can be found online at
wsupress.wayne.edu

MEET BEHIND MARS

STORIES BY RENEE SIMMS

WAYNE STATE UNIVERSITY PRESS
DETROIT

ISBN 978-0-8143-4512-2 (paperback)
ISBN 978-0-8143-4513-9 (e-book)

Library of Congress Control Number: 2017962356

Publication of this book was made possible by a generous gift from The Meijer
Foundation. This work is supported in part by an award from the Michigan
Council for Arts and Cultural Affairs.

Wayne State University Press
Leonard N. Simons Building
4809 Woodward Avenue
Detroit, Michigan 48201-1309

Visit us online at wsupress.wayne.edu

For my parents, Ralph and Elaine Richardson,
and my children, Ava and Amir

Contents

High Country

On the day before the last day, Hathoria Vernon considers a new idea. She tosses around the possibility that her novel-in-progress sucks. The celebrity author who flips through her twenty-page excerpt implies as much. "I don't know Hat," he says, in a pose of writerly solidarity. "I just feel there's no room for aporia in your tale. It's too focused and the young girl is so heroic." He stares at the surface of a latte as he speaks. She wonders if that word, *aporia*, is an omen, a linguistic hoodoo that he's pulled out of his coffee. She nods as if she understands while studying his facial hair. His beard glistens like it's been brushed with baby oil. When her turn is over, she counts how many women writers hover in the Hilton banquet room waiting to chat with this guy. Thirty-five, at least. She looks up the word *aporia* when she returns to her hotel room.

The agents at the Ocean View Literary Conference point to other problems with her 600-page novel, about a girl coming of age in 1980s Detroit:

It isn't Romance.

It lacks drugs, sex, hip-hop, guns.

Believability! Black kids blissed-out on German disco? What was this, magical realism?

Hathoria is bone-tired by the end of the conference. She spends the last day curled in her hotel bed with her "Hello My Name is Hattie" name badge in a lanyard around her neck. Hattie is the name she goes by and the name she'll use when she publishes, whenever that is. In choosing the name Hathoria, her parents were not trying to be mean. They were sixties intellectuals. They named her after the Egyptian goddess Hathor, the goddess with the head of a cow. Curled in the sheets, she thinks of this: Jervis paid a thousand dollars for her to fly out to Pacific Palisades, he will want a full report of the conference, and what can she say? Although she's enjoyed the food and the bougainvillea-laced landscape, she leaves feeling less like she's gotten advice and more like she's just been hustled.

She feels fat.

"What did they think?" Jervis asks when he picks her up at Detroit's International Airport. "Are they going to publish you?"

"They didn't like it."

"Why not?"

"It's a long story," Hattie says. She decides that she's intended this pun. "How are the kids?" she asks.

"They missed you."

"Where are they?"

"I paid Kim to watch them this afternoon. But, baby," Jervis continues, "I can't believe they didn't like your story." He adds an old school "Chumps!" as his final comment, which reminds Hattie why she still loves this man.

They walk past a line of rumpled travelers waiting to get through airport security. People look demoralized; it shows in the way they shift as they stand, in the way they kick their luggage on the brown-speckled floor. One woman is so pissed that she's yelling at three uniformed TSA officers. Hattie gathers that the woman has had a bottle of designer perfume seized by security.

"Ma'am," the TSA officer says to her, "liquids can only be three ounces."

The woman accuses them of seizing only the luxury items. "What happens to my perfume once you've got it?" she asks. "This cologne cost two hundred twenty-five dollars with tax, and I know y'all don't just throw it away!"

Hattie wonders why a person who can afford two-hundred-dollar perfume hasn't taken more vacations and isn't acquainted with the flight rules. But she realizes that her question is a dumb one. The woman is like everyone else, a worker who has spent her week's pay on merchandise to convince herself that life isn't crap. It's been four years since Hattie worked. Initially she stayed home to raise their young kids, but now her reasons have changed. Although she and Jervis have not discussed it, Hattie stays at home to prop up their myth that Jervis's income alone is enough.

After a walk that seems without end, Jervis and Hattie emerge from the concourse and baggage claim to enter the maze of the parking structure. Jervis has parked at the outer edges as usual. After another long walk, Hattie finally sees the bulging curves of her husband's Ford truck. He's parked on an angle and far away from neighboring cars so that no one can nick the exterior.

They travel the I-96 and John C. Lodge freeways in silence. Jervis plays with the satellite radio and checks his online navigation system. Hattie eats two packages of Red Vines that she purchased during her layover in the Dallas airport. Later, she'll remember some article she read about red dye #40 reducing brain weight and vaginal patency in laboratory rats.

A month later, as they vacation in Arizona, she thinks about her novel. As she rides in their rented minivan, Hattie stares through the window, imagining. She asks herself questions that she's read in writing books on craft, like, What does the protagonist want? What are the protagonist's fears?

They are in Phoenix to visit Jervis's mom, but they have also planned to drive to the northern high country for some time at a mountainside resort.

"Look alive!" Jervis says, startling Hattie. She's ignoring him again.

"What is it?" she asks.

"Earth to Hat," he says. "Come in, Hattie, come in."

She exhales. "I'm here," she says flatly.

Her twins, Malik and Maya, are in the second row, throwing raisins into every upholstered crevice of the rented van. Malik is the child with the good looks, the lashes and thick hair, while his sister struggles to grow a decent ponytail. But Maya has strong traits of her own; she is smart with a mouth on her. This, Hattie believes, are the best qualities for a girl. Hattie's youngest son sleeps soundly in his car seat. His nickname is Freddie Jackson. Freddie's big head drops to one side.

"Is your mother watching the kids when we drive up north?" Hattie asks.

"She can't," Jervis says. "She's in a golf tournament tomorrow."

"How are we going to relax if the kids are with us? How am I supposed to write?"

Jervis runs his hand over the shiny bulb that is his head. He's losing his hair, and in preemptive lawyerly style, he shaves his head bald before the hairline gets the best of him. Hattie has noticed other signs of aging on Jervis, like his rounding gut, but she never complains. She's fifteen pounds overweight herself.

"I asked you to check with Kim," Jervis reminds Hattie, "to see if she could travel with us. Remember?"

Hattie cocks her head to the side. "Who was going to pay for a *nanny* to fly out to *Arizona*?" she says. "We have to stop wasting money like that."

This time it is Jervis who exhales. "I don't know how else you're going to find the time to write," he replies. "I was going to bring Kim out here for you."

Writing had been fun when Hattie, at thirty-three, first took it up. She had been the most outspoken member of her book club; her co-members deferred to her close readings and highbrow interpretations of the novels that they read. It didn't matter that for each selection, Hattie would read every critical review she could find online, from the *New York Times Book Review* to *Kirkus Reviews*, and then repeat those opinions as her own. Nor did it occur to the other women in the club that Hattie's understanding of plot and themes were culled from her perusal of *SparkNotes*. Just as the book club women deferred to her, Hattie deferred to the book experts. She never questioned a critic or *SparkNotes*, and as a result, never developed her own sense of what worked and didn't work in a novel. Now, three and a half years after being encouraged by others to write—"Hattie you should write!" "You should do it. You're a *writer*." "Girl, you'll be famous"—Hattie understood that she didn't know how to build a novel's infrastructure from the ground up and word by word. Hell, she hadn't even known the definition of *aporia*! Her manuscript was a wasteland of half-formed ideas. The writing workshop she took at Oakland County Community College only confused her more. The writing instructor had mastered one response—a slight smile, as if she'd just smelled oven-baked cookies—while the participants, other late-in-life writers who knew less than Hattie about writing, waited their turn to make snarky remarks about the manuscript up for review.

"You should turn your novel into a vampire story," a retired electrician had told her.

Mama Vernon meets them on the patio of the Horsethief Pub & Grill. It's a restaurant inside of a golf club. The walls of the restaurant are painted the color of cantaloupe and honeydew melons. The patrons, including Jervis's mom, are retirees who dress in the latest golf attire. Mama Vernon has just finished nine holes and she wears a yellow dress that shows off her toned legs. She is a well-preserved woman who loves a dirty joke. During lunch, she talks about her neighbor who ran over his wife with a golf cart.

"Don't you repeat this," Mama tells them, "but he don't seem cut up about it at all."

"How did it happen?" Hattie asks.

"He was backing up, didn't see her, and get this—the cart didn't beep. That's what you call a design defect, right Jervis?"

Jervis is in Ford Motor Company's products liability legal group. He pushes a forkful of chicken burrito into his mouth and chews. "Dempfemt," he says.

"What he say?"

"He said, *depends*," Hattie explains.

Mama leans in close to Hattie. She says, "One of the retirees published a poem in the *Sun Lakes Gazette*. I'll get her number so you can talk to her. She might give you some advice, you know, about publishing."

The exhaustion Hattie felt at the writing conference returns. She's aware of her lack of concentration during lunch and the tightening muscles in her neck. Her vision starts to blur. It occurs to her that she might be crazy, that her eyes and mind are betraying her. She experiences a swift panic, a feeling she's had in the past when she's noticed a stray dog that has spotted her first. She begins to sweat and she gets a nose full of her own armpit odor. She makes a fuzzy mental note: Tom's Natural Deodorant does not work in the desert.

As her peripheral vision goes dark, Freddie Jackson leans over and nuzzles her breast. He wants to nurse. She places his head beneath her shirt and he latches onto her nipple, stinging it. This sensation and the feeling of calm that follows it is rooted in her affection for her hungry child. She thanks God for the reptilian brain! She's still functioning. She hasn't completely unraveled.

After lunch, they drop Mama off at her retirement community. The squat tan and olive houses look like tortoises lined up close together. Mama's house is no different than the others. It's tan, with rocks instead of grass, and a clay-tiled roof. The ceilings are high, which gives the illusion of more space than there really is. Jervis's mom doesn't need much room because she lives alone. Mr. Vernon died years ago.

Mama fumbles with the keys as she lets them inside. She goes immediately into her kitchen and to the "goodies" cupboard above her microwave.

"Now don't eat all of this at once," she tells the kids as she hands them peanut butter crackers and a box of Nilla Wafers. "It's for your ride to Sedona."

The kitchen is black and tan like the rest of her house. Mama's instincts are to blend southwest and African motifs in her furnishings and in the way that she dresses. At church on Sundays, she wears headwraps made from mudcloth and chunky, turquoise jewelry. "You're so stylish," the other retirees tell her. To Hattie, the woman looks like a mash of ethnic confusion or a Pier 1 Imports store.

The kids are already opening their snacks and pushing bright orange crackers into their mouths. Mama Vernon watches Hattie, and when Hattie looks up to acknowledge that she's being watched, her mother-in-law smiles sweetly. "How was your conference?" she asks.

"It was okay," Hattie says. The twins are chasing each other using Hattie's body as their object to run around. Occasionally they step onto Hattie's feet. "Ouch, stop it," she says. She is watching Freddie pull himself up on the couch. She's worried he might lose his balance and tumble backward onto the glass coffee table.

"Did you sell your book?" Mama Vernon asks.

"Not yet."

Jervis stands up from the couch and lifts the baby into the air. Freddy arches his back and squeals. "She's almost there, mama," Jervis says. "This time next year, Hat will definitely have a book."

He walks over to Hattie and kisses the top of her head.

"We better get on the road," Hattie says.

Malik and Maya run to the front door, leaving the wrappers from their devoured snacks on the kitchen counter and floor.

"Bye, Grandma," the kids say as they leave.

"Bye, babies."

Mama Vernon walks with them out of the house and into the stultifying heat. She takes a position on her rocks near a leaning saguaro. She is a blur of brown and yellow as their minivan pulls off.

"I don't want to do the tourist stuff," Hattie tells Jervis.

They've started the two-hour drive to Sedona, but their check-in is four hours away, so they're discussing what they'll do to kill time. Hattie knows her comment annoys Jervis since he loves all things vacation.

"That's fine," he says. "We can drive to the Hopi reservation and look around. Maybe after that you'll be grateful for tourist stuff."

"Hopi reservation?" she says. "You know how to get there?"

He holds up a map of the Sonoran Desert.

Freddie Jackson nurses in her lap in the front seat. It amuses her how much the baby resembles his R&B namesake. Hattie hears the twins arguing and biting each other in the second row. She turns around in her seat and slaps their knees with her free hand.

"Stop touching each other," she says. "I mean it."

When things quiet down, she buckles the baby next to the twins. She listens for his heavy breathing, which will mean that he's asleep and she can steal a few moments to think through her novel. If she can find the strength, her story is on the verge of breaking open and revealing the world exactly as she sees it. These are the moments that she lives for though she pretends, especially at Ford Motor Company parties, that she lives and breathes for her family. Hattie pushes back into her seat and attempts to get comfortable. She tries to think of how to complicate her novel's heroine. She watches the sky, which is close, seeming to rest on top of the earth.

"Have you revised any of your novel yet?" It is Jervis's loud voice once again.

"When have I had time to write? When I was packing sippy cups and potty seats?"

She hates that she is bitter. She hates even more that Jervis has become a bullying writing coach. It happened once Freddie was born. As their family has grown, their money has gotten funny, and her husband's interest in her writing career feels mean. Like he really wants to tell her to make money as a writer or go back to work.

"Eeeeeww," Maya says. "It stinks in here." Malik quickly joins in. "Freddie pooped! Freddie pooped! Freddie pooped! Freddie pooped!"

Hattie climbs into the second row and puts her nose to the baby's diaper. He's done a number in his sleep, or in the restaurant, or at his grandmother's house—who knows?

"Want me to pull over so you can change him?" Jervis asks.

"No, I don't want to wake him up for that," Hattie says.

"He shouldn't sit in that stuff," Jervis says.

"He's fine."

Jervis looks over his shoulder at the baby. "I'll pull over, it's not a problem."

"I said I don't want to wake him."

"And I don't want to smell you-know-what for another hour."

"I don't want to smell you-know-what either," Maya says.

They are at the edges of the reservation, driving through miles of vacant land. Every half-mile, they pass a house that has tires weighing down its tin roof to protect the shelter from nature's whims. Hattie returns to her seat. They drive by a house with a cage in the front yard. The cage is constructed with branches and rope, and inside there is a large eagle. As they pass, the bird sits up and spreads its wings. Hattie is watching the bird when a group of kids run in a zigzag formation toward the van.

"Watch out for the kids!" she says.

"I see them, Hat."

The children carry bundles of wood carvings in their arms. Jervis accelerates the van so that the children never get within yelling distance.

"Jervis, can you slow down?"

"Mommy, Maya touched me!"

"He touched me first!"

"Be quiet," Hattie says. "Jervis, can you slow down?"

"I'm not driving that fast, Hattie."

Freddie wakes up and begins to cry. Hattie climbs again into the second row. She lifts the baby from his seat. She is about to unsnap his pants when the van jerks, throwing her into the back of the passenger seat. She hears Maya's screams. Maya sounds like the monkey in *Faces of Death*, the one that is clubbed by restaurant patrons who will later eat the animal's brains. Hattie hasn't thought of this movie in years. In college, she made a weekend ritual of getting high, watching the movie, and laughing at the wasted lives. Hattie lifts her head to see Jervis looking ahead with his eyes wide open. Through the windshield, a hazel-eyed cow turns to look at the family. It gives them a lover's wink as the van drives into its side.

Suddenly, the animal disappears. No, they're climbing over it, crushing cow bones into the earth. The van rocks at extreme angles, its center of gravity now gone. Hattie listens to the screaming of her children and the awful lowing of the cow. Eventually the van is forced like the bovine onto its bulbous side.

Had this scene been workshopped at the community college, the retired electrician would have asked two questions: Can a van climb a cow? Do cows low or moo?

●

When Hattie wakes, she is riding in the flatbed of a pickup truck. There are two men, one slim and one rotund, riding inside the truck. A woman rides next to Hattie in the truck's bed. She has broad cheeks, a white afro, and she is missing one of her legs. "I'm so tired of riding," she says when she notices Hattie staring at her. "We need to stop for a minute. Aren't you tired of riding?"

The woman turns to the men inside of the truck. "Hey!" she shouts. "Let's stop at the Prickly Pear!"

The truck pulls up to an adobe building without a door. It's dark inside. Hattie can smell cigarettes and stale beer. This smell also brings back memories from her college years when the bars had the stench of yeasty ale absorbed into the wood floor. She wishes she'd known then what she knows now, that the college years are as good as it gets. If she'd known this before, she would have taken on more lovers.

The skinny guy gets out of the truck. He wears a straw hat and his narrow face ends in a scraggly-haired chin. He has a moustache with hair so sparse, it isn't worth the trouble. The man throws a brown prosthetic leg onto the flatbed. "Put your thing on," he says to the woman. He looks at Hattie. "You hit that cow hard," he says. "Cows are so dumb." Hattie watches the woman strap the leg onto her stump and scoot to the edge of the bed. The man helps her to the ground and then holds her as she walks.

"They don't move," he continues. "That's how stupid they are. They just stand there. And at night out here, man, you can forget driving fast. Those fuckers stand around in the pitch black and if it weren't for their eyes, you wouldn't see the fuckers. You'd nail them every time."

"Their eyes?" the woman says.

"Yeah, their eyes glow in the dark," the slim man says.

"No they don't," the bigger one says.

They tell Hattie that they are brothers. The woman is a friend of theirs.

"Don't you want to rest?" the woman is asking Hattie. She is walking in a hop-clump fashion as the smaller brother holds onto her waist.

"Where is Jervis?" Hattie asks. "Where are my kids?"

"At the res hospital," the skinny one says. "My name's Wynn, by the way. This is Arleta and that over there is Marlin."

"Can you take me to the hospital to see my children?"

"In a minute, sugar," Arleta says. "Let's sit down and have a drink first."

Marlin takes ahold of Hattie's arm as they walk into the Prickly Pear. It isn't a bar, as Hattie had initially thought, but a store with Kokopelli wood carvings similar to the ones the running children had cradled in their arms. Behind this room is another room. Hattie sees people back there smoking and drinking beer. She tries to free her arm from Marlin's grip but he holds tight. She looks at him. He's six feet four inches tall, at least. He's browner than Arleta, but with straight hair that he wears in a ponytail.

They walk past a blond woman with rugged skin who appears to be the store's proprietor. She waves as they pass by her to enter the second room. In the corner of the room is a bucket with bottles of beer on ice. They sit down. Marlin grabs two beers in each hand and brings them to their table. Hattie begins to cry.

"Oh look, honey," Arleta says, "things could be worse."

"What happened to my family?"

"They're gone," Arleta says. "Isn't that what you wanted, sugar? For them to be gone so that you could write?"

Hattie stares at Arleta. She is aware of the heat again and of the sweating that she can't control. A ceiling fan whirls above, moving the dusty air around.

Arleta takes a swig of her beer, then lets out a loving belch. "I've been waiting for you to write me into one of your stories," she says. "Look—my hair turned white I've been waiting so long."

Marlin snorts.

"She don't write about people like you," Wynn says. "She's a classy lady."

"Look who's talking. You and Marlin ain't been in a story for years."

"That's not true. Marlin was in that Sherman Alexie story."

"Oh, that's right—when was that, 1992?"

Marlin drains his beer in a noisy guzzle. Arleta places her moist hand over Hattie's. "Look, I need work," she says. "I'm tired of being around characters waiting for a gig. These people get funky when unemployed."

"Who gets funky?" Wynn asks.

"Whatever," Marlin says.

"You all are characters?"

"Well, of course, honey," Arleta says. "And I want you to know I can play a young girl or young woman, whatever you decide."

"You can't play no young woman," Marlin says. He and Wynn start to giggle and Marlin gets so tickled, he places his head face down on the table to laugh. Arleta rolls her eyes.

"Marlin, I *know* you're not laughing," she says. "Somebody has to write about Sasquatch before you'll get any work."

All three of them laugh now; it's a cackling that sounds like explosives.

"Is my family at the hospital?" Hattie asks.

"Is my family at the hospital?" Marlin mimics.

"Drink your beer," Wynn says.

"No," Hattie tells him, "I need you to listen to me."

Arleta flicks dirt from beneath her fingernail. "That's not what we do, sugar."

Marlin goes to get more beer, but when he discovers that there is none, he lifts the metal bucket with ice and throws it against the wall. Cold water splashes on the men who are sitting nearby and they fly out of their seats and begin fighting him. Marlin wrestles two men at once. They thrash about in the water and knock over chairs.

Wynn watches the scuffle. "Bad behavior," he says, shaking his head. "That's why it's so hard for my brother to get work. Louise Erdrich wrote him into a sacred scene at a sweat lodge and Marlin throws a Coors onto the stone pit. Erdrich highlighted his paragraph and deleted the whole thing out."

Arleta touches Hattie's upper arm. "I want to be in the story about the girl from Detroit," she says.

"I'm about done with that story," Hattie tells her. "I can't make it work."

"I want to be the character who owns the jazz bar where the Techno deejays hang out. The one who dances and kicks her legs between jazz sets."

"Come on, you can't play that role with one leg," Wynn says. 'What happened to your leg anyways?"

"I lost it in a Flannery O'Connor story."

"Dude, I heard she was rough with us," Wynn says.

Hattie is crying again, big ugly tears that wet her shirt. And her breasts are leaking milk. Clearly, her breasts weep for Freddie, her missing baby, but why is she crying actual tears? Is it for her failed novel or for her family? Maybe this has been her insanity the entire time: she cannot love both equally. Her cheeks feel hot with shame as she realizes which commitment she will abandon. "I'm having a hard time with my novel," she says. "I was hoping for some inspiration in Sedona. Jervis had read about the vortexes here."

"Yeah, that's some gringo tourist bullshit," Wynn says. "No offense."

"Why don't you write while we're here?" Arleta asks. "Write for a couple of hours and then we'll take you to the hospital."

"But I don't have paper or a computer."

"Think-write," Arleta says.

Arleta and Wynn leave the table and join people who are sitting nearby. The proprietor comes in and tells them to "Keep it down! I have a tour group shopping up front!" No one listens. Hattie sits alone with her bottle of beer. The drops of water on the glass are cool. She runs her fingers across the bottle's wet surface and watches Marlin lift a man off the floor by his neck. The man's face turns the rough red of a pomegranate. The man's friend hits Marlin across his back with a chair. Hattie can hear bits of conversation from the other tables. She feels the whirl of the fan as it moves the heated air. Her breasts have engorged with milk and feel as big as human heads. She wonders how much pain she would endure by staying where she is. Her milk would eventually dry up. Her anxiety might even go away. More and more, she tells herself, *Hattie, you will adapt.*

Dive

We'd been traveling by car for five and a half hours, I-75 north stretching before us like a parched riverbed. I looked over at Roman, whose eyelids were low. "Want me to drive?" I asked. He ran his hand over his mouth and grunted in response. When I asked again, he responded, "I'm fine. I got this, Alex."

It was just like Roman Abelard to hold fast to the driver's seat. He was young then—we were both in our early thirties—and being the leader in our relationship made him feel like he was in control. It didn't help that I was seven months pregnant with his child. My new physical condition clearly made him nervous. And it gave him reason to boss me around.

"You just relax and take care of the bambino," he said, smiling. He tugged at my braided extensions with his free hand.

"Professor Abelard is going to be a great father. You watch!"

This is what my student, the one with the crowded teeth, told me. She was in my first year composition course that year, one of six sections that I taught between two universities and one community college. She was also in Roman's Introduction to Poetry. Intro to Poetry was one of two courses that

Roman taught each term at City College, Miami. He was tenure-track there and I was not. "Roman cares," this young woman told me that day. I had no idea how she knew that Roman and I were a couple, and I felt chagrined that she would chat me up about my love life—in the hallway, no less. But I didn't complain. I was contingent faculty and too scared to have students dislike me. So I simply nodded. I agreed that Professor Abelard knew a thing or two about empathy—and he does! Roman's poetry describes how hard it is to be black, immigrant, and male, and (God bless him) a couple of his poems contain a few ideas about women. Yet, his sensitivity doesn't come from writing poems, but from having survived a bad childhood. Roman is kind to people because he was *that* kid: the nerdy boy who was dressed in secondhand clothes. The one who spoke with a thick accent. Roman knows what it means to be heckled by teenaged shitheads.

"When my dad left, I put on thirty pounds within a year," he told me on our first date. "I was twelve years old, so you can imagine how that went at school."

As we drove I-75, the corn fields of southern Ohio passed outside the windows. In three hours, we would cross the state line into Michigan. At the boundary, the sign that welcomes travelers to the Great Lakes State would rise from gravel near the highway's edge. Nothing else remarkable would be anywhere nearby; only cornfields and a farmhouse that looked, from a distance, like a crumbling pink cardboard box.

Cornfields and flat roads never inspired feelings of greatness in me. This was one reason why I left my home state. The land never made my eye wander upward toward any goal. As a girl, I kept my eyes peeled at the horizon and what I saw there—slow-moving bodies and gray skies—filled me with a quiet dread.

I also left to figure out who the hell I was.

At eighteen I moved away from Tiny Oaks, Michigan, boarding an interstate bus that smelled like it had never been cleaned. I arrived days later in Miami. Now there was a landscape that rolled, that had spatial density and fast-moving cars! I decided to stay put. I found part-time jobs in hotels, at Mucci's Gelato, Publix, Target, and Magic City Casino. When I was fired from these jobs, I partied full time with my friend Yesenia, then a coke dealer, then crack addicts (in that order), before finishing grad school in creative writing when I turned thirty-two, teaching as an adjunct, and finally getting clean.

Four miles past the pink farmhouse, a ravine emerged with a brown creek rippling at its bottom. This brought to mind the creeks and lake that ran behind the home of my adoptive parents. Roman and I were traveling the interstate to visit them. It was daddy's seventieth birthday and my mom had planned a big party and invited all of their friends. Daddy was a fourth generation Ramsey, from Atlanta, Georgia. He was also the first person in his family to graduate from college, from Clark College, now Clark Atlanta University. When I was a girl, Daddy was a big deal wildlife biologist. He'd spend hours at the creeks and lake behind our home, collecting small life forms from the dirt, and trolling the lakebed to look at aquatic plants.

I distinctly remember the morning he pulled me from watching Saturday cartoons and said, "Put your shoes on. I want to show you something down at the lake."

"But I'm watching *Fat Albert*."

"I know. I need you to see something. It won't take long."

I side-eyed him. I slid on my Buster Brown shoes with my flannel pajama pants and clomped behind my father. We headed out of the sliding glass door to the stained deck and then down to the edge of Pine Lake.

"Daddy, I'm missing my show."

"Sssh," Daddy said, "Look over there." He pointed at a clump of tape grass shooting out of the water. I bent forward and squinted until I saw clearly what was next to the grass: one wood duck and its duckling, a waterfowl and its chick. The baby birds were nudging each other and flapping their fragile wings. Big fucking deal, I thought.

"I've seen these birds before," Daddy said, "but I don't know how in the world they ended up together as a flock. The ducks are native, but the fowl—God bless them—they keep getting pushed farther north and I'm not sure why."

I kicked at a pile of washed-up seagrass on the shore and daddy squeezed my upper arm.

"Alex, you've got to be still to observe."

I bit my lip and tried not to wriggle. I had fifteen minutes left until Mush Mouth, Weird Harold, and the rest of my favorite television characters would disappear from the screen until the following week.

"Look at that!" Daddy shouted. "They're moving together like one family. Isn't that something?"

"Yeah," I said. Then I turned and ran in my big hard shoes back into our house.

Drunk and high years later, I said this to Roman: "I think my father dragged me out there that morning to have our only conversation about my adoption. You know the whole 'every-family-is-different' talk. I mean, think about it. My parents adopted a five-year-old girl from foster care and brought her into their interracial middle-class world. Even though they never said so, they had to be scared as shit."

Roman, who was sober, and eating lemon cake, looked at me across his kitchen table. It was scattered with crumbs. "Let me see if I understand what you're saying," he responded. "Your father tried to explain why he adopted you by showing you two ducks and some fowl?"

I remember the two of us sharing a fit of giggles sitting there at his kitchen table. I love how logical Roman can be, especially for a poet. And of course my sober self doesn't believe that was Daddy's sole motivation. What I didn't appreciate as a girl, or in my drugged-out days, was that Daddy was not just any biologist, but an often-cited black biologist in the early 1970s. He had published over a hundred journal articles. He knew the intricacies of the Great Lakes ecosystems. He knew the species of all indigenous fish, knew the two hundred varieties of aquatic plants in Pine Lake. He knew when the mating season for the bluefish began and ended, and he knew the gestation period of the black-headed gulls that nested near the lakes. He had taken me out to the lake that morning, not to talk about my adoption (that was wishful thinking on my part), but because wildlife was my father's *first* love. It was how he had found meaning in the world and how he'd created a secure life for himself. Daddy once told me that many of the answers to life are right there in the lake.

It was dark when Roman and I finally drove into my parents' driveway. He turned off the ignition and we sat in the darkness. Roman stared out the windshield at the two-story colonial. I turned awkwardly in my seat and fished with one hand for a package in the back seat.

"Oh, fuck," I said. "Where's the present?"

"Calm down. It's in the trunk," Roman said.

We climbed out of his Camry like sailors discarding their sea legs, which is to say *slowly*, especially for me. The weight of pregnancy grinded upon my ankles and knees. I'll never forget that pain. The skin on my feet had ballooned while we drove. I could barely stand outside the car without feeling like the skin on my feet might burst. Also, as I walked, I felt mild cramping across my uterus.

Roman grabbed onto our suitcase and I grabbed my purse. Roman fetched the wrapped present from the trunk. I crumpled our fast food trash and candy wrappers into a tight ball that I held in my hand as we trekked up the driveway to the front porch.

I'd forgotten how eerie nighttime is in townships like the one where my parents live. There's a reason why so many horror movies have had suburban settings. I dare you to look out at night at the expanse of an unlit backyard and not see eyes lurking in the hedge. If you've ever had to listen to your drunken neighbors curse each other out after a day spent grilling pounds of meat and drinking cases of beer, you know the mainstream menace of which I speak.

Roman rang the bell twice. He turned to look behind him a couple times as if he were spooked. When no one answered, I tried the brass knocker. The vibration from the knock traveled up my arm and settled into my teeth.

Soon, a light came on and then the door opened. Daddy leaned his bald head between the door and frame. His navy blue bathrobe was belted at the waist. "Alex?" he shouted. "What in the world?"

"Happy birthday!" Roman and I shouted together back at him. I clawed the trash ball in my hand.

I wish I could say here that Daddy whisked me into his arms and kissed my face. That he shook Roman's hand and welcomed him into his well-lit foyer. But let's be real, that's not who my family has ever been. After Roman and I shouted our greeting, we were motioned inside, but we all stood there not speaking, our arms dangling at our respective sides. Finally, I threw my arms around Daddy's neck. He leaned slightly into me and placed one hand on my back. Just as quickly as we touched, we both let go. When his shoulder bumped my hand, the trash ball fell onto the marble floor.

"I thought you were flying in tomorrow from Miami. Is that your car? You all drove?"

"Yes, we drove. We wanted to surprise you."

"Well," Daddy said, staring at my protruding belly. "I'm definitely surprised."

My mom hung back in the foyer, having let my father answer the door at this hour when decent people in their small township were asleep. "You *are* pregnant," she said. "Come on in, let's see you."

I stood under the chandelier so she could step back and take a full look. Her eyes were cloudier than I remembered. I tried to picture her as a young schoolteacher. As the woman who vowed never to let her body be used to reproduce. The firebrand with the attitude and greasy hair. Then I tried to imagine her years later, once she decided to marry my dad. He convinced her that they should adopt, and when she told him that she wanted to adopt me, this cemented her reputation as a radical woman in their circle of friends.

"This is Roman," I said.

My mom stumbled for words. "Welcome, Roman," she said. "Nice to finally meet you and congratulations."

"Should Elizabeth warm some food for you?" Daddy asked. "Are y'all hungry?"

"We'll probably just turn in," Roman said. "It's late and we've been driving for half of the day."

"Let's have some dessert," Daddy insisted. "Don't we have pie in there, Elizabeth? We should have something we can offer them."

"Alex should probably lie down," Roman said.

"Let's talk first. You like pie, Roman?" Daddy asked, causing Roman to flinch. I wondered whether Daddy, a keen observer, could sense Roman's complicated history with food.

"Yes sir, I do."

"Then let's all sit down and have some dessert."

"Can't we eat in the morning?" Roman asked.

When Daddy finally backed down from his invitation for midnight pie, we climbed the stairs to the second story. Mom followed me and Roman into my old bedroom.

"I was going to change the linen in the morning. I didn't expect you here tonight."

"Mom, that's fine. We're so exhausted we don't care about clean sheets. Trust me. It's the last thing on our minds."

She looked hurt. I was too exhausted to figure out why.

"Well, you know where we keep the sheets if you change your mind."

"I'm just gonna take a warm shower and fall into bed. I'll come down to your room and say good night before I do."

When I emerged from the shower stall, Roman was already fast asleep in our bed. He was spread-eagle on his back and snoring. He'd left no room for me. It was one of those moments when the past and present converged and time felt like a loop. Here I was back in my childhood bedroom with a snoring man whose tired legs dangled off of my twin bed. I was reminded of how good I'd had it as a kid living in this big house as an only child. How I'd have to make room, somehow, for a grown man and a baby. I went down the hallway to my parents' bedroom. "Knock-knock," I said outside their door.

They were sitting there on the bed with their backs to each other. Mom patted the space beside her and I sat where she instructed. "How is the pregnancy going?" she asked.

"It's incredible," I said, "and a bit ridiculous. I mean, look at me. I'm huge, but I'm feeling pretty good."

"You're not tired?" Daddy asked with an edge in his voice.

"I am."

"Why are you having a child, Alex?" my mother asked. "You just recently got your life together."

During the months I'd spent going to Narcotics Anonymous meetings, I'd been taught the value of speaking about my desires. "Say what you want," Ms. Katrina would scold me. That is not something I learned growing up.

"I want Roman's baby," I said, "and I want someone who looks like me. I've never had that before."

Daddy cleared his throat before he spoke. "Roman seems nice. A bit protective."

"He cares," I said, stealing the corny words I'd heard my student say.

"I see. I suppose that's why you're with him, because—." Daddy stopped short.

Instead of completing his thought, he stood and started turning back the bedspread and sheets. He climbed into their huge four poster bed.

"Because what?" I asked. "I'm with Roman because he *feels*."

Roman's breathing had settled into a deep but quiet sound when I returned to our bedroom. I thought about sleeping on the floor, but decided to nudge him instead until he rolled over and made room. He turned onto his side and I squished against him, staring up stupidly at the ceiling. I could never drift off to sleep as easily as him. Plus, it was hard to position my pregnant body comfortably. I imagined our little fetus floating in its sac of amniotic fluid, oblivious to me, or Roman, or to its anxious grandparents sleeping down the hall. I imagined it floating in its pre-world, a world of water and sound. Then, before I drifted off, my thoughts moved to the summer that Daddy taught me how to swim.

We were out on the sailboat all that year. I'd just been adopted and Daddy was frustrated that I was not grateful for my new home. For this opportunity to swim in a lake.

"I never had to learn how to swim where I lived before," I said, referring to the foster home.

"But you're here now," my father answered. His belly hung over his plaid swimming trunks. He scratched a space right above his navel.

"Why do I have to swim?"

"Because you're here," Daddy said.

This was his imperfect logic, but he stood by it. I was going to learn to adapt—he was sure of it. Since he studied the lake and I lived with him, I would learn how to study the lake too. He planned to take me down to the lakebed to introduce me to the aquatic world. This idea of being in the water terrified me.

In fact, I liked nothing about that damned lake. Not the way it smelled. Not its amphibian color. The first time I went out on our boat, I vomited up the spinach dip and crackers on which we'd been snacking. Then I cried.

And I have never shed dainty tears like some sweet frightened girls. Instead, I howled and blew snot. I shook uncontrollably. Mom said I cried like a person clawing her way out of a grave.

"Oh my goodness, Alex," she once said to me. "You cry like there's no one in the world who loves you, my dear."

"I want to go back to the dock," I pleaded that first day on the boat.

We were stalled in the middle of the lake. There was no land around. I could feel my heart squeezing up into my throat.

"You'll get used to it," Mom said. She rubbed my five-year old back. "Pretty soon you'll love being out here. You have to challenge yourself, Alex. You can do this."

But I couldn't imagine getting used to sailing. All that damn rocking! And I couldn't imagine liking the creepy lake. My heart would race when I simply dangled my feet from the pier. I'd think about all the creatures writhing in the lakebed silt, never seeing daylight.

"I am not at all curious about what's down there," I told Daddy. That's how

I talked as a little kid. Daddy was sitting on the deck smoking a cigar. He squinted at me as if he were trying to figure me out. Those light brown eyes in his dark brown face seemed beyond my knowing and wisdom. The only thing I could tell was that he was exasperated by my little girl drama.

So in August, he threw me into the lake.

I recall that moment in slow motion. The way the sky melted into the treetops as I plummeted. "Pretty poetic for a grumpy fiction writer," Roman told me when I described the memory to him. I remember all the bubbles and the burn inside my nose.

"Move your arms, Alexandria!" Daddy shouted to me from starboard side. "Kick your legs and move your arms!"

I remember my terror as I sank. The water rose around my face. I flapped wildly about, trying not to breathe in the lake water. Daddy stood there, unmoving, like a punishing god. That's how I remember it, but my years in therapy and recovery have taught me not to trust all my memories as facts. The truth is that at some point, Daddy leapt into the water and saved me.

Eventually I would learn how to swim.

Then Daddy would insist that I learn to dive.

The morning of Daddy's birthday, Mom was the first one awake. When I came downstairs, she stood in the kitchen spooning the yellow filling for deviled eggs. There were vegetables on the counter. Party decorations crowded the kitchen table next to a large cake that was still in its box. On top of the cake in blue icing it read, *Happy 70th Birthday, Wild Bill!!!*

"Do you want me to slice these veggies in the food processor?" I asked.

"No. You start decorating the house. I can handle the stuff in the kitchen unless you really want to do it."

I spent the morning dusting, polishing, and hanging sparkled banners. I swept the deck where, Mom said, her guests would dance all night to music.

I frowned. "What music you plan on playing?"

"Our music. Nancy Wilson. Lou Rawls."

I laughed. "Okay. Who did you invite?"

Mom began a long conversation about the Shultzes and the Browns. Edith Long was bringing her son, Edward, and Edward was bringing his family. She asked if she had told me that Edward had a wife and daughter. That they bought a house and blah blah blah blah blah?

"Yes, seems like you told me that a while ago," I said.

Mom stayed in the kitchen and only came out to spy on me. She didn't trust me to work consistently. She and daddy had an old school work ethic. They hunkered down on whatever task was at hand and they shut out everything else. Work, work, work—that was them! They were the perfect role models of their generation. They believed in silent suffering, "bootstraps," and suburbia. Mom's family had been working-class Jewish, but we rarely saw them or Daddy's family from Atlanta. This infuriated me. I wanted us to slow down, to bring our many histories with us. But my parents only looked to the present world they had constructed for themselves. That left me with what I liked to call my Trifecta of Absence. I had no ancestral information as an African-American. As an adoptee before adoptees had rights, I had no knowledge of my biological family. And I had sparse knowledge about Bill and Elizabeth, the kind but unemotional people who'd raised me up.

Mom handed me three bouquets of flowers that she'd been keeping in her garage refrigerator so they would stay fresh. She said I should feel free to put them wherever I deemed best. But as I walked toward the bar, she cut in front of me, protesting that choice.

"Maybe put those flowers on the coffee table, here," she said. I did as I was told.

"Have I told you that Dr. Davis retired to Sarasota? He went down there maybe six or seven years ago. Last time we spoke—well, your father was the one who spoke to him—but the last time *Bill* spoke to Dr. Davis he had grown disenchanted with the place. He said the crime rate was starting to rise. Not sure what that means. In any case, how is your teaching? You must have a really diverse group of students. A lot of immigrants, I bet."

I arranged a group of lilies and irises in another crystal vase. I placed these flowers on the end table near the couch.

"Yes, my students are diverse. That's what I like about Miami," I said. I continued, uneasy with who my mother had become in her older age. I was annoyed by her use of the word diverse, which meant my students must be black and brown. And this from a former schoolteacher. I changed the subject.

"Freshman composition is a throwaway course. I want to teach literature but my position is not a real position. You know this, right? That Roman is the one with the real job?"

Mom tilted her head slightly as she looked at the flowers on the coffee table.

"Have you and Roman talked about baby names yet?"

"Not really. We're getting to it, but there's just so much to do."

"Sure," Mom said. "I understand. There are lots of good names in your dad's family, you know. Like his aunt Myrna. I've always loved that name, Myrna. I have good names in my family, too, but not as many. Oh! But I'm being presumptuous. Roman probably has his own family names that he's considering—no?"

"No, not really," I said. "Mom?"

"Yes, dear?"

"We're planning to find my biological family once the baby is here."

My mother considered this for a moment. "Have you told your dad about these plans?"

"No, not yet. We will," I said.

"Well, good luck with that. You know how your daddy is."

She motioned for me to follow her. "Before I forget, I want to show you something downstairs. You're going to love it," she said.

We walked downstairs into the basement and to the cedar closet along the far wall. When Mom swung open the door, I saw my dolls from years ago, seated in rows on a shelf facing forward. All of the dolls had been restored.

"Oh my god, they look so good!" I said.

"Your dad would not let me throw them away. I was trying to clean up around the house, you know, just clear out some of this junk we've had forever. But he said 'No, hold onto Alex's dolls,' and so I found a place on Orchard

Lake that restores old baby dolls."

I looked at the mostly brown dolls that sat perched on the cedar shelves. I couldn't wait to pass these dolls on to my own child one day.

"Some of them were a real mess," Mom said. "You'd drawn on some of their faces and some of them had that matted doll hair, you know, hair splayed all over their heads, but this shop—Carol was the woman's name—Carol replaced some of the hair and she found clothes for those that were without them. It cost me a small fortune, but she did a great job."

I praised all of the detail on the new doll clothes. "She did a fantastic job," I said.

"I was pleased," Mom remarked. "She took longer to finish than she'd promised, but when I saw the end result, I was pleased."

The men slept in until late morning. When they awoke, I heard their muffled conversation through the floorboards. They stayed upstairs, laughing. When they came downstairs an hour later, they walked shoulder to shoulder.

"I was telling Roman about the mink that's living up shore about two miles," Daddy said. "It's the first one we've seen in several years."

"Because of climate change," Roman added. Roman would always move through life like a favored student. He spoke as if he'd taken notes from their talk upstairs.

"And some of our neighbors want it trapped," Daddy said. "The mink has been stuffing Craig Anderson's sump pump with dead frogs that it's killed. Storing them there. If I can catch it, I'll give it to the county forestry department and maybe they can transfer the mink to an area that's less populated."

Roman poured himself a cup of coffee. He sat at the kitchen table and leaned back in his chair. He winked at me. It was nice to see him concerned with something other than the pregnancy.

My dad continued. "Roman wants to see the mink, so we're taking the boat out. Elizabeth and Alex, you're welcome to join us."

"We're getting the house ready for the party," Mom said. "We don't have time to go out on the boat."

"We won't be gone that long, trust me, Elizabeth."

Roman came over and cradled me in his arms.

"You don't have to go if you're not up to it," he whispered in my ear.

"I'll go," I whispered back. "It might be a good time to tell my father the news."

That summer that I learned how to dive, Daddy insisted on perfect forward lunges. High arcs, head down. Slice through the water without a lot of splash.

"Why does it have to be perfect?" I protested.

"Just listen, Alex," he said. "Pay attention."

Later, I'd learn that he'd taught himself to dive as a soldier during the Korean War. Most of the white soldiers knew how to swim and many of the colored troops did not. During their off-duty time, this difference was just one more thing for a black soldier to be teased about. And so my father set out to obliterate the distinction.

I attempted dozens of forward dives that year. Each time, my heart heaved up into my throat before I leapt. Each time, I smacked the water with my face, belly, and legs.

"Jump off with your feet as hard as you can," Daddy would shout. "Bend at the waist and hold your head down for Gods' sake!"

Over and over I dove into the water. My nose burned from the lake water that would leak into my nostrils as I descended. I went down so many times that I ended up with swimmer's ear. Only then was I allowed to take a break.

"You're pushing her too hard," Mom said when I cried about the pain in my ear.

"She'll be alright. She's a tough girl," my father said.

But this was not true, I was not tough. If I am tough today, it is after years of being told that's what I am. I am tough and resilient, adaptable. I can do it. By the time I was ten, I could no longer remember a life that didn't include swimming in a lake. I spent hours during my childhood sailing Pine Lake and Lake Michigan. I spent even more time underwater with daddy, searching the sediment for clues about our lake's inhabitants. I learned to hold my breath longer than anyone else I knew; so long, in fact, that I became the champion among the neighborhood kids. I went undefeated in our underwater competitions. I could hold my breath longer than any child should. I never kicked up to the surface to gasp for air. I could hold my breath to the point that most people would black out.

We sailed on the windward side of the lake for forty-five minutes without sighting the legendary mink. Roman spotted a nest made of twigs. "That nest is probably constructed by the mink," Daddy said, but the weasel was nowhere to be found. The sun slowly cooked us overhead. After an hour of this, we were all pretty drained.

"Well, we should probably head back," Daddy said.

Even at seventy, he was a strong captain, navigating the waters with confidence. He turned the boat leeward so we could go home. He had spent the entire time talking to Roman about conservation success and its link to demography. For the most part, he ignored me and Mom, but I didn't care. I enjoyed watching Roman and Daddy bond.

Daddy looked over his shoulder at some point to where I sat. "How are we doing?" he asked.

"Fine," I said. "I'm ready to head back to the house."

"I think we're going to make Roman into a man of the sciences," Daddy said. "He's going to leave the humanities and come to the other side."

"You mean the dark side?" I joked.

"No, I mean the side of objective truth," Daddy replied.

Roman laughed and reached into the picnic basket for a ham sandwich.

"Speaking of the humanities," I said, "Roman's first book of poetry will be published this fall."

"That's wonderful. Congratulations, Roman," Mom said.

"We hope that this gives him some traction in a job search. We'd like to leave Miami eventually. We'll relocate here if he can find a job at a local university. If we come here, we'd search for my biological family."

"Why would you do that?" Daddy asked.

"Why would I get in touch with my biological family?"

"Yes."

"To learn my genetic background," I said. "Surely, *you* understand that."

Daddy's back was to me as he guided the boat. I wanted him to lock the steering wheel, tack, and let the boat sail itself. We had the wind at our backs and Daddy knew this. He didn't need to guide the boat. He could tack and turn around to face me as we talked. I waited patiently, but he never turned around.

"You should leave it alone," he said to me over his shoulder. "Those people gave you up for adoption. You might be inviting trouble by seeking them out."

"But—"

Roman squeezed my knee and shook his head. I read his gestures to mean, "Let it go." I did as he instructed, but I was furious the entire ride back home. What would it have cost my father to admit that he and Mom had been wrong? They'd raised me to believe my personal history didn't matter, that I could make it without knowing my past because I was strong. For too many years of my life, I nearly killed myself in service of that belief.

Guests began arriving for the party at four o'clock. "Happy Birthday, Bill!" echoed all night through the house. Most of the guests were my parents' age. They asked me obvious questions over and over. What was I doing now? Did I like Florida? When was the last time I was home? I didn't know how much my parents had shared with them about my recovery, and so I kept my responses simple. I was teaching college, I said. "A college professor," they would say and I'd think, *Yes, something like that.* I told them I loved Florida, but I missed Michigan. I wanted to be closer to home. I told them that I had not been back for a couple of years.

When I found myself alone, I looked at my watch. There were at least four more hours of daylight before it would be dark. I had been on my feet for a long time that day. I remember that I felt a bit dizzy.

I was sitting down and rubbing my feet when Edward Long arrived. He came with his wife and two-year-old daughter.

"Alex!" he said. "It's really good to see you. Congratulations on your pregnancy."

Eddie's daughter stood there hugging her father's leg. She wore a white sundress and she had a dozen butterfly barrettes clipped into her hair. She remained quiet and attached to her father for several minutes, but then, once she got a sense of her surroundings, she began running through the house in between all of the guests. She tried to reach for one of the vases of flowers. My mom swooped in and caught her just in time.

"I bet you'd like a doll," I said to the little girl.

I walked slowly down the basement stairs to retrieve one of the restored dolls. When I handed it to Eddie's daughter, the girl's mouth fell open. She clutched the toy to her small chest. "Baby look like me," she said, and began running again through the house.

After everyone had consumed too much gin and deviled eggs, mama asked me to carry Daddy's cake onto the deck. She picked up a spoon and began clinking it against the side of a glass.

"Can I have everyone's attention," she said.

I placed the cake on a long wooden table. I inserted the candles—a seven and a zero—and lit them.

"Can I get you all to move out to the deck?" Mom asked.

Slowly, the conversations ended and people gathered outside around the cake. There was late afternoon sun on the lake and it was just beginning to get dark. The candles on the cake flickered, casting shadows.

"*Happy birthday to you . . .*" Mom began to sing.

The guests joined in and sang the most drunken, off-key version of the song that I'd ever heard. It was charming because it was so odd. After we sang, Daddy pushed his chair back and stood. He cleared his throat.

"I want to ask my family to come forward," he said.

Roman raised his eyebrows at me from across the deck. I shrugged in response. Do as we're told, my gesture said. Roman got up first and I followed him. We walked to Daddy's side. Mom was already standing next to him.

"Our daughter came home last night," Daddy said. "She and her—ah—"

"*Partner*," Roman whispered.

"She and her partner, Roman, drove all the way from Miami to be here. They're expecting their first child," he said, "and Elizabeth and I couldn't be any prouder."

Then in front of his guests, he pulled me close and kissed my cheek.

I probably would have stood there in shock for the rest of the evening if it hadn't been for the splash. We all heard it, and then the loud screams. Eddie and his wife were running to the end of the pier. Their daughter had thrown the baby doll into the lake and then fell in herself as she tried to retrieve it.

I kicked off my shoes and started running.

"Alex!" my mother called to me from the deck. "Don't go in that water!"

Roman says that I looked hilarious as I ran. He said I resembled a car that had heaved up onto its rear wheels to drive. He says that my "struggle-sprint" is why our daughter, Myrna, decided to exit my body early. Each year on her birthday, we share this story with her.

"Alex, don't do it!" I heard Roman say.

I lumbered to the edge of the pier and then stopped at the end. The wooden planks were warm from the sun, but the breeze was cool and I shivered. I sat on the edge of the pier. I clasped my hands over my head, leaned forward, and dived in.

I felt the cramping in my midsection almost immediately, but still I swam to Eddie's daughter. She was just starting to go under. I grabbed her around her small waist with one arm and then side-stroked back to the pier. She was crying, but she would be okay. Eddie and his wife were just as frightened as their girl.

"She's okay," I assured them, as I steadied her on the pier. "She's gonna be okay," I said again.

When I saw that Eddie's daughter was safe, I turned around and dove back in. My body felt heavy and amniotic fluid must have leaked from my body as I swam.

The lake was not as green as I remembered. Maybe it never had been green, or perhaps, as Daddy liked to say, "This is how global warming looks."

The dried-up creek beds and sparse aquatic life. I saw no traces of lake cress, or plankton, or ground fish. There was only clear water for miles, which made it easy for me to spot the baby doll on its back. I stretched out my arm and kicked my legs. The toy was right within my reach.

The Art of Heroine Worship

It was 1977 and cider mill season, and Lottie Roberts was the tallest girl that I knew. Well, maybe not *the* tallest. Tonya Jackson was taller and wider, but she didn't count because everyone knew that Tonya was not really one of us. She didn't live in our neighborhood but was using her grandmother's address in order to attend our schools. So excluding Tonya, Lottie was the biggest girl in my sixth grade world, and that seemed right since Lottie's reputation was oversized as well. Her legend grew as she grew. The biggest rumor that year was that she'd lost her virginity to the dope dealer's son, to a boy named Eldred Lumpkin.

Kids skipped the Lumpkin house on Halloween. We were scared the SweeTarts his family passed out were in reality small tablets of LSD. But someone said they saw Lottie eat the Lumpkin candy and that Eldred gave Lottie poems he'd written in red ballpoint pen.

Parents wanted to believe that Lottie would be a loose woman. It only made sense, they argued, since her daddy was an ex-Motown singer. She'd spent her formative years on tours all over the world and surrounded by the debauchery of the music business. It was "Lottie's lot in life," they said, coveting the sound of alliteration on their tongues. Some gossiped that her mama wasn't her real mama, that her real mother had been a precocious teenaged fan.

"Plus," they said, "the girl is too pretty for her own good," and certainly that was true. We'd noticed fathers in our neighborhood glancing sideways at her.

By comparison, Tonya was only noticed for not being pretty enough.

"You *so* black," this one boy said to Tonya, "your blood type is burnt positive." Everyone walking home from the bus stop that day dropped to the ground and shuddered with laughter.

I never defended Tonya from these neighborhood taunts. I didn't want her dark skin and coarse hair, her grandmother-as-caretaker, to be traits that kids associated with me. But I did defend Lottie. "Leave her alone!" I would shout. Inevitably, some kid would clap back, "Just shut up, Marie." I would be rich today if I had a dollar for every time I heard, *Shut up, Marie,* or this: *No one was even talking to you.*

I defended Lottie because I loved her. It wasn't sexual, but it was romantic in the way that young girls worship each other. Lottie was my idol. She had traveled out of the country and she befriended whomever she pleased, people like Eldred Lumpkin. Her life was too large for our cloistered Detroit suburb. I wanted to believe that the same was true for me.

But in the fall of 1977, our neighborhood's obsession with Lottie pushed her away from our community for good. It began when we learned that our neighborhood would be bussed to a new school. The school was near Ten Mile Road and the students there were mostly white.

We heard it first from Filene. A group of us were standing between her candy-striped swing set and the dog pen that housed her family's German Shepherd.

"You guys are going to JFK in September," Filene said.

"How would you know?" Lottie asked.

It was a good question. Filene, her brother, and her sister didn't go to school with the rest of us. Filene went to a private girls' academy, which was fifty minutes outside of our town. At six-thirty each morning, she boarded an abbreviated school bus, the kind that seated maybe a dozen people. She rode to a school that was miles from our neighborhood.

"My mom told me," Filene said. She stood up on one of her swings and began to pump herself while standing up.

"How does *she* know?" someone asked.

"Her mother's a city council member, stupid!" Lottie said.

Filene pumped herself higher and higher until her swing set started to shake. She talked to us over her shoulder. "Yep, that's how I know. The city council had to approve it."

Later, Mama would say that the politicians rezoned our school district to counteract our migration patterns. She and Mrs. Middlebury laughed about this as they stood in the yard one afternoon.

"Too many of us moving in here, especially around Eight Mile. They have to shake it up a bit," Mrs. Middlebury said. As she spoke she laughed in that way that I hated, the way that exposed the gaps between her side teeth.

When I was in fifth grade, Mrs. Middlebury scolded me and Lottie for playing "Run and Go Get It" with Marcus and Dwayne. "Girls, come here," she called to us from her front porch. I ran to where she stood, but Lottie just walked slowly while twirling the ends of her hair.

"I want you to know I saw y'all kissing those boys, and I'm very disappointed in your behavior. Good girls don't neck out in public," she said.

Mrs. Middlebury didn't have children of her own, but she had three miniature terriers who yapped at us from behind her screen door. As we stood there that day, the old people smell of her house wafted through the screen mesh.

"Stop doing what everybody else does," she said, looking each of us in our eyes. "Marie, I know *your* mama has taught you better," she said to me. She glanced out the corner of her eyes at Lottie but said nothing about her mother or upbringing.

When we were finished getting dressed down, we walked back over to where the boys were.

"What did she want?" Marcus asked.

"Nothing. Nothing at all," Lottie said.

Then Marcus and Dwayne both slapped at Lottie and pulled at her long braids. In the back of my mind, I knew the game had been a competition for

Lottie's attention, but I'd been included nevertheless. I hated Mrs. Middlebury for trying to take even this from me.

Walking into JFK that fall was like walking into the wrong family reunion. I had never heard of the food that was served in the school cafeteria. In my house, Mama cooked sweet potato pies that she cooled near the kitchen window. She made pound cakes with whole bags of C&H sugar. Who in the world ate stroganoff and what was an apple crisp? In music class, we did bouncy European folk dances and sang nineteenth-century songs.

Then there were the hallways at this new school. They were narrow, and each day they smelled of the wood pulp and detergent that janitors put down when someone threw up.

But worst of all was recess. This is when our neighborhood had the hardest time trying to blend in. Some of us made friends by playing sports, but many of us, like Tonya, were always alone, digging in the dirt or watching other folks play. Lottie made friends easily. She played with girls who invited her to swing or to braid their hair down their back like hers.

"I hate this white school," I blurted one day at recess. I said it out loud, but to no one in particular. Tonya looked up from digging in the sand.

"I dare you to say it louder," Lottie said to me. We were near the tether ball court. There were lots of kids around.

"I'm not saying it louder."

"You scared?"

"No.

"Then say it."

"*You* say it."

"I hate this white school. Now, *you* say it."

"I hate this white school."

"Say it louder."

"Lottie, stop playing around. I'm not saying it again."

A girl who overheard us told our teacher, Mrs. Levy, so after recess our neighborhood was pulled out of class and into a smelly hallway to be identified.

The girl who told on us stood in the hallway, crying and wiping her nose. I could not understand what upset her. It wasn't personal. No one had said anything directly to her.

"Who said it?" Mrs. Levy asked, and the girl pointed squarely at me.

"No I didn't," I whined, but that's all that I said. I looked at Lottie, who stared malignantly at the girl. No one else said a word. Mrs. Levy looked at me, then at Lottie. She gave our entire group a lecture about unity. When she finished, there was a pause like someone should clap, but instead we walked back into the classroom to learn.

At the end of seventh period, Mrs. Levy asked me and Lottie to hang around for a few minutes. We watched other kids file out of the classroom while we sat at our desks waiting for whatever.

Mrs. Levy had wide hips like parentheses and frosted blond hair. I liked her. She introduced me to the word *gentile*. That's who she was, "A gentile who married a Jew," she said. In class, she riffed about Judaism and her in-laws. Being different from her family amused her. It was easy to distract Mrs. Levy from the lesson plan and into a comedy routine about her family. She was hilarious, but I was never caught laughing at her jokes out loud.

Mrs. Levy sat behind her plywood desk reading and writing on a stack of papers. Without looking up she said to us, "Quick, tell me one thing you like about school and don't mention me, that's a given."

That was Mrs. Levy. All wit.

"Three-twenty p.m.," Lottie said.

"That's funny," Mrs. Levy replied. "Do you think you'd like it more if you were involved in after-school activities?"

"I don't know," Lottie said. I shrugged my shoulders.

"The music department is staging a production of *The Sound of Music*, and instead of waiting until the spring, we're going to do it earlier this year, like in a couple weeks. You girls should audition. Who knows? One of you may end up playing Maria."

She was still bent over the stack of papers, slashing the pages with a red pen.

"Think about it," she said.

I looked at the top of our teacher's head. Her hair was an unnatural color except for the shiny black roots. I said something like, "Maybe we'll try out," then Lottie and I ran to catch our bus before it left.

The front half of the bus was filled with white kids. Most of them lived near the school and their bus ride home was ten minutes, max. The back of the bus was loudest; that's where our neighborhood rode for half an hour. We were crazier, all of us, than we'd ever been before. On the surface, our schooldays at JFK were no different than our days at the old school, but if you looked closely at us—on the bus, in the lunchroom or playground—you could see that our lives had been turned upside down and we were trying to figure out what it all meant.

The kids in the front of the bus watched and listened to us, especially when they pretended not to. That day, some girls from our neighborhood began a rhythmic stomp and clap. Then came the chant, *My back aches, my pants too tight, my booty shakes from the left to the right.*

The chanting continued until we reached our subdivision.

Most of the parents in our subdivision had been born before 1950, somewhere in the south. They were from towns like Mobile, Decatur, Little Rock, and Meridian. They'd moved to our suburb when they were fully grown and could pay their own way, as Mama liked to put it. They'd been told that spaces were so wide in our town that their closest neighbor would be a field-holler away. If they'd been living cramped in city housing for any length of time, that openness appealed to them. So did the Levittown-inspired circularity of the streets. Our subdivision had three streets that were formed like a no-entry symbol. Westhaven turned into Westpoint and back again, and through the middle ran Westwood Place, the shortest street, and the block where my parents' house stood.

Through my school bus window, I could see the black diamond shapes that my father had painted on our garage door. My father painted with a hand that was missing two fingers. He'd lost the fingers in an accident at work. Daddy believed back then that he would one day be an artist when he stopped working as a millwright for General Motors.

He and Mama would not be home when I got there. Their shift ended at four-thirty and they didn't get home until an hour after that. I could not have friends over to visit when they were not at home, but I could go outside to play as long as I didn't go far.

That day, however, I stayed inside. I searched my closet for what I would wear at my audition.

It turned out that pretending came naturally to Lottie.

"Close your eyes and see yourself as someone else," she said.

We were in her bedroom where light came through her window in fat, amber stripes.

I closed my eyes and imagined myself as Lottie. My dark, limp braids became plump, reddish ones. I was cute and all the boys liked me.

"Now open your eyes," she said, and I did.

"Now close your eyes without closing them."

"That doesn't make sense."

"Just try it, Marie. You're always so scared."

"I'm not scared, it's just that what you said is impossible to do. You can't physically close your eyes without closing your eyes."

"No, dummy, just pretend to close them but keep your eyes open. Imagine you're someone else with your eyes open."

I tried doing what she described, but it was hard pretending to be Lottie when the real one sat right before me.

I wanted to ask her if she had ever daydreamed about being someone else because I couldn't imagine who else she would rather be. But I never got up the nerve. Instead we talked about the musical and practiced singing songs.

Only a few students tried out for the production. I was chosen to play Louisa, a part of no real consequence, but Lottie got the lead role as Maria. Another kid from our class, Kevin, was chosen to play Captain von Trapp. Lottie was not happy about her kissing scene with Kevin. She said Kevin tasted things that he pulled from his nose.

Kevin, Lottie, and I got to skip fifth period each day to rehearse. We practiced for the musical in a room adjacent to the gym. We each took one corner and a record player and rehearsed our parts. Kevin used the time to quickly read his script, and then the rest of the time he read comic books. After the first week, I did the same. I quickly read my script, and then cracked open a new novel.

But Lottie always practiced. She put the album on her record player and she danced around the room, memorizing. She danced around the room as if she were alone, imagining her blue dress and her Julie Andrews hair. As she danced and did those deranged hillside twirls, Lottie Roberts became Maria.

My mother invited everyone she knew to our evening performance and everyone politely declined. Only my mother's mother, Mimi, said she would go. Before show time, we drove to Detroit to pick her up. On Seven Mile Road, we passed ten churches and thirteen KFCs. I counted. Mama looked pretty; she wore a blue dress and gold earrings that dangled. Daddy wore an ascot, and because he used his clippers that evening, his afro was more halo than hair. He didn't say anything, which was his way, until our car bottomed out in a large pothole. Then he barked, "They need to fix the roads in this goddamned city." Mama turned from the front seat to smile at me.

"I'm so proud of you," she said.

At Grandma Mimi's house, her husband, Leon, was on the porch with the man who lived above their flat. They were drinking whiskey from waxed paper cups. Mama went into the house. I ran and jumped into Leon's arms and inhaled the musk and cigarette odor that lingered in his mechanic's shirt.

"I hear you in a play," he said, grinning his stained tooth smile.

"Are you coming?" I asked.

"No baby, Leon has to be at work at nine-thirty. But do me proud."

His smile stayed wide as I slid down and out of his arms.

"What role you playin'?" his friend asked.

"Louisa," I said, "but my friend Lottie is playing Maria."

"Maria? Which play is that?"

"It's a musical," I said.

"You know, the musical the sexy dancer was in," Leon said. He listed slightly to the left. The porch banister pressed into his leg. "God! What was her name . . . real sexy woman . . ."

"Sexy dancer?" the friend said, then spit into the hedge. Mama and my grandma came out of the house and descended the porch stairs.

"Real pretty legs," Leon murmured, "fine, *fine* woman with sexy legs."

"I'll be back around nine," Mimi said.

"Moreno! Rita Moreno."

"Rita Moreno," the friend laughed.

"No," I said in my expert voice, "Rita Moreno played *Anita*, not Maria. That was *West Side Story*. We're doing *The Sound of Music*, and Maria is an Austrian nanny for the von Trapp family."

"Lord," Leon said to Mama's back, "y'all gon' fuck this poor girl up."

At the end of the evening performance, the parents all stood and began a frenzied round of applause. Lottie got the loudest applause for her portrayal of the black Maria, and lots of smiles like she'd performed an amazing trick. As I walked through the gymnasium, I spotted Mrs. Levy talking to a parent. When I passed by them I heard Mrs. Levy say, "Yes, well, we wanted to do something early, you know, get the kids used to each other."

After her lead role in *The Sound of Music*, Lottie was chosen to join the girl's choir. Everyone agreed that she was a talented singer, maybe as good as her father. It was not so much her tone but that her interpretations always involved risk.

The Sound of Music was the beginning and end of my musical career. When it was over, I joined the newspaper club and yearbook club. Words were how I best expressed myself, not in conversation, since I was too shy many times to speak, but on paper I was confident and could express anything at all.

A month after the evening performance, we did the musical for the students. There were paper wads thrown, catcalls, and straight-up laughter when

Kevin and Lottie kissed. I remember looking out at the audience during my brief moments onstage. No one was really paying attention. Tonya sat in the front, heckling us the loudest, but she sat alone without any friends around her.

"Hey Lottie," this boy yelled to her on the bus ride home, "what's Kevin taste like? Vanilla?"

It was Indian Summer and the leaves were like flames on each branch. I admired the trees through the bus windows as we rumbled through town toward Eight Mile Road. Lottie sat in the seat across from me. She sat alone, her legs stretched over the length of the seat, her feet dangling into the aisle.

"*The hills are alive,*" someone sang. Everybody laughed.

Lottie's celebrity status at this new school had the kids on edge. It was okay when she was just *our* Lottie Roberts to talk about, but in this new environment where we all struggled to be recognized, something about Lottie's acceptance inspired the cruelest envy.

Lottie rested her head against the windowpane, her nose in the air. Behind us, kids swapped seats and popped sweet-smelling gum. Conversations mixed with the roar of the bus engine.

Tonya came from the back of the bus to whisper something to the one girl who would talk to her in public. As she walked up the aisle, then back down, she bumped Lottie's feet. Twice.

"Watch where you're goin'," Lottie said.

"What'd you say?" Tonya asked. She stared at Lottie over one shoulder.

"I said, Watch where you're going."

"What you gon' do?" Tonya asked.

People started to kneel on the seats to get a better view of their exchange. The edges of windowpanes started to fog.

"Sit down," the driver warned. She stared at us in her mirror. This was her first day on our route and already she looked worn out. She had facial features that were bunched like a bat's and bulging forearms that suggested repetitive motion.

"What you gon' do?" Tonya asked again. "You need to sit in the front of the bus with the other white kids."

People tittered into their hands.

"And you need to sit your fat ass down."

"Why don't you make me, ho?"

Within seconds the tension had reached this point where words could no longer express emotion. Lottie leapt from her seat and Tonya turned to face her. They were the two biggest girls and they fought with closed fists. But on that day, punches were not enough. Lottie's hair must have looked too tempting in the battle. Her fat braids flying into the action must have reminded Tonya that, unlike Lottie, she'd always be the girl who was ignored, the girl whose her hair would be a mess because her grandmother couldn't plait it or straighten it sufficiently, and it was like a pile of blackberries on her head, a twig of one-inch braid on top.

Tonya grabbed Lottie's hair and pulled. Tufts of dark red hair floated to the floor. Each day, we played the dozens and teased each other relentlessly, but I had never been in a real fight. I tried to pull Tonya off Lottie, but I was jabbed by an elbow in my temple. I tried again. I grabbed Tonya's arm, which set her off balance, and when that happened, Lottie pushed forward and tackled Tonya onto the floor.

Before I knew it, Lottie stood on the edge of one seat and began stomping Tonya in the face. Tonya's nose bled and her eye would be swollen shut. Her blood smeared for inches along the white sole of Lottie's gym shoe.

The driver stopped the bus and marched towards the back. She pivoted her hips in order to fit through the aisle. Someone opened the emergency door, and one by one kids jumped from the exit laughing, cursing, and discussing the blow-by-blow details.

Before I jumped, I stood motionless, unable to turn my head from the violence before me. Lottie brought her foot down again and again on Tonya's head. Lottie struck Tonya without pity or celebration, much like a factory machine that cannot detect the presence of human fingers.

When I saw that the driver was close enough to grab us, I found the courage to speak.

"Come on, Lottie!" I said, "Come on!"

We ran to the exit and jumped off the bus. Once on the street, Lottie bent over with her hands on her knees and breathed through an opened mouth.

"Anybody else want some?" she asked.

We were at least five miles from home.

The Cows of Lantau

You've agreed to lead the conference call this one time. The purpose of these conferences is to plan your 30th high school reunion. You live in a different time zone from the other callers. It is the middle of the frickin night for you. *Hello?* you say after the beep. You repeat hello and state your name, a small hassle.

Oh, heeeeeey, the collective voices holler back. *We were waiting for you.*

Well, here I am, you say. *Wait no more.*

You hate that you are still sassy Party Girl after all these years. It's like being a hostess at Applebee's your entire life. You blame yourself. For craving male approval. For never breaking with the known script. You've been playing this role since the first phone conference, when a classmate asked why you live in a rural village near the South China Sea. *Well,* you'd said, pausing to think of an answer. *I'm here for the wealthy bankers in Hong Kong, of course.*

Tonight, as leader, you ask, *So who do we have on the call?*

The creepy guy from your class speaks up first. If anyone bests you at playing the role assigned to them during high school, it's this dude. You remember his tight posture as he strode the hallways in his ROTC uniform. *I've been married to the military for thirty years*, he enunciates on the first call. *I majored in Homeland Security.*

Who else is on the call? you ask tonight, and one by one each caller says her name.

There are seven Reunion Planners, six women and the military man. You are all people of color. The white people in your class have seemingly disappeared.

The graduating class of your Compton-area high school was 727, and now some of you are no longer alive.

Good to hear everyone's voice, you sing into your phone. You're faking your perkiness. It's three a.m. and you feel like the low-lying fog that fumes across the island. The Merrill Lynch financial advisor you followed to Lantau Island last year broke up with you to live with a woman in the Red Light District.

You type on your tablet the names of those present for the call, creating conference notes to distribute later via email. Your signature block will read Rochelle Ellis, English Instructor, Primary School, Mui Wo, Lantau Island, Hong Kong. The Planning Committee will respond promptly to your email. They will offer cordial suggestions and *thanks so much!!* The other emails will all have their own signature blocks with fancy titles and company names. *Okay*, you say, *we have one agenda item. Do we want a seated dinner or strolling food stations?*

You met the financial advisor in an L.A. bookstore in the dystopian fiction aisle. He smiled and found creative ways to look at you from all angles. You fell for it. You hated your principal at the school where you taught anyway, so when the advisor asked if you would relocate with him, you left the states to explore Hong Kong. You wanted to try something new, but have you really done so? You have another teaching job. You've learned how to kill snakes with a machete. And ride a bike on dirt roads. You've also learned how to catch ferries and where to buy a good pollution mask. You've learned how to fetch water from the bottom of a well and you've grown accustomed to spotting buffalo. You're learning how to be alone now that the financial advisor is gone.

The Reunion Committee decides to go with food stations. People socialize better when they walk to retrieve their food. Someone agrees to look into an eighties D.J. Someone else will contact that famous classmate who sings R&B. *And does anyone know how to contact that guy who is a Hollywood actor?*

Outside your window you hear roaming cows, which scares the shit out of you. Boats knock against the rotting wood of the pier. You get up and pull your window shut.

You heard the cow myth soon after you arrived as an expat on the island. Locals like to tell the story.

It begins with a rancher who wasn't from the village, because who among them would think to tether cows together at night? Those who knew the man said that he believed roping the cows was a good idea, believed it was the perfect compromise between the practices he knew from home and the traditions here. He said in his country cows were placed inside stalls, though he acknowledged the cruelty of factory farming. *But here you let the cows roam*, he said, *which isn't bad, but the cows can get lost at night.* People who listened to the man would correct his thinking. *Roaming is not a problem*, they would say, *because cows only move during the day. At night, cows stand still, their breathing barely audible.* But the rancher insisted that his cows roamed at night. And he designed something like rope except it wasn't exactly rope or chain, but a glittering braided leash that he used to link his cows together by their hooves and the scruff of their necks. You've never confirmed the story, but this you know is true: at night there's an awful lowing across the village. It sounds like animals stumbling and dragging each other through the dirt.

It sounds like death, if you are honest, and at your age, death chases you each night. Stares at you from each mirror. You've lost dozens of friends, classmates, both of your parents, a brother, an uncle, two aunts, cousins—and on and on and on. All of the good rock stars died at your age (or shortly after reaching fifty) and like them, you are tired. For years, you were tired of the herd; you tried without success to be singular, unique. Now you're tired of difference. Tired of change. Tired of apps and Quick-Pays and online outrage. Sick of endless chatter, of work, and it is not the thrill of food stations that compels you home to L.A., but the desire after all these years away to acknowledge the common binds between you and former classmates.

Someone suggests T-shirts for the reunion. And a class donation to the school. What about a tour of the high school for the committee? To see what it looks like today? And what about party favors? Or a softball game? What about accommodations for people who want to bring their kids?

You type all of their ideas, which you will shape into a structured document and send to each member of the committee. *Anything else?* you ask, your finger poised above the end button on your phone. When there is silence, you conclude the call.

It's almost dawn where you are. Later, as you take your morning walk, you will pass a group of men in dark suits, lining up for the ferry that takes them to work on the mainland. You are not going to work today. It's the Lunar New Year, a national holiday for everyone who is not a trader or broker. As you walk, you see boats tethered to the pier. Their knocking against the wood is less troubling in daylight.

The Australian broker flirts with you as you pass the ferry. This time you stop and talk to him. You give him your number. You feel his eyes on your ass as you leave. Your old habits are so hard to break.

For laughs, you type a list of Future Agenda Items. The list makes you think through the decades. It helps you consider what you and your classmates might yet have in common:

Committee for DHS Reunion, Class of 1984

Future Agenda Items

1. Regarding Our Classmates Who Are White: Do They Even Plan to Show Up? (discussion)

2. The Classmates We Lost to Gunfire (compile list)

3. What *Was* School Integration? (discussion)

4. The Classmates We Lost to Cancer (compile list)

5. How We Survived the Reagan Years (a prayer circle)

6. A Remembrance of Michael Jackson (PowerPoint presentation during reunion dinner)

7. A "Prince Was Always Better" Retrospective (competing PowerPoint on opposite wall)

8. Let's Talk About the "Fast Track": Who Knew and Who Had No Idea? (discussion)

9. Why Do We All Have the Same Middle-management, Upper-management, and Government Jobs? (a research committee)

10. Our Classmates Who Are Locked Up (PowerPoint)

11. The Classmates Who Lost Their Homes to the Foreclosure Mess (a GoFundMe account)

You read your list that you've typed onto your tablet. Your eyes sting because your eyes are old.

You think, *What would it mean to break free?* Then you reconsider, positioning your finger above *Send.*

The Body When Buoyant

Because her court-appointed therapist had suggested it, Nichelle began solving crossword puzzles. She liked the ones in the alternative weeklies the best. The average time she would spend on a puzzle was twenty minutes, but her best time had been twelve minutes, seventeen seconds, forty-six words. After she finished that puzzle, her mind began its usual drift. Thinking that she needed more puzzles to distract her, she bought a book of crosswords that she began carrying with her to work and on the bus. She solved puzzles in between her errands for Frank Yee and as she rode the Metro to his house, but she also opened her book each night when she returned to her brother's home. The letters she pencilled into each square were uneven because her hands shook. Today, she had passed an hour on a crossword, a good deal of that time on one tricky homophone. Frank had watched over her shoulder as she parsed through the clues. When she finally figured out the word that had stumped her, she wrote it down in her unsteady hand.

"What's c-a-r-e-t?" Frank asked.

She pointed to a picture of the noun in her dictionary.

Who had ever heard of caret, not to be confused with carat: the weight of a gemstone, or carrot: a root vegetable? Nichelle felt let down when she read the definition. Her mystery word was a symbol that meant "insert here."

"Disappointment is normal," her therapist liked to say.

What was not normal was standing outside a stranger's house and pressing your face against her window. This is what Nichelle had done. This is why she went each week to talk to a therapist. Before committing this act, she'd walked past the gingerbread Victorian many times. She'd taken in every detail on those walks—the rock gnomes planted in the herb garden, the olive tree in the front yard, the bougainvillea's horizontal march across the back fence. But on that day, Nichelle had not been content to just look. Instead, she pressed her face to one of the windows and saw that the new owner, a young white woman, stood near the brick fireplace.

The interior of the house looked exactly as Nichelle had imagined. The glass was cool on her forehead and she pressed into the coolness. Her breath fogged the window, allowing her fingertips to slide easily on the glass. She turned her head and placed her cheek against the condensation. She closed her eyes. She moved her fingers in arcs across the window until her pinky finger hit a chink in the glass and she opened her eyes. A crack shaped like a spider had pricked her skin. She applied pressure to the crack and then a little bit more. She remembered the ripping sound and the look on the woman's face when the window broke.

"You leaving for the day?" Frank asked.

She stuffed her puzzle book and dictionary into her black duffle. "You know it. But I'll be back on Wednesday."

She had the easiest homecare client in the world. Better than her friend Cathy's. Cathy had been assigned to a sick man who bit her as she bathed him in a tub. Nichelle didn't have to help Frank get dressed or anything. There was nothing really wrong with Frank. He was just old and his eyes were growing dim.

"I'll need to get a haircut on Wednesday," he said.

She stopped at his door, her duffle bag swinging from her shoulder. "Alright then," she said. "I'll see you when I return."

Before her life had become what it was, Nichelle was living with her mother. The two of them shared a walk-up in Orleans Parish. It was right after Nichelle's divorce. She and her mother were grudging roommates, her mother reminding her each day that her ex-husband "ain't never been shit." That Nichelle had been the one taking care of *him*.

"I'm taking care of you now—what's the difference?" Nichelle said.

The day they moved in, she carried her mother's shoes, all twenty large boxes, up the stairs in soaring heat to their flat. On good days there was a breeze that would catch through the screened windows and move through the rooms. Most days it was a sweatbox up there, especially when her mother turned on the oven which she seemed to do every day.

"Why can't you just cook on the stove?" Nichelle asked.

Her mother did many things that vexed her, like drink bourbon through the night. And she had a habit of lining objects into rows or heaping them into piles. Her junk took up much needed space on their floor and counter-tops. She'd cluster spoons, jelly jars, pencils—you name it—but it was the shoes that drove Nichelle crazy because there were so many of them. One night, Nichelle came home to find her mother on her knees rearranging the shoes and other clothing by color. Red shoes went with red hats in one corner, and so forth. "So," Nichelle said. "What you doing now?"

"What it look like I'm doing? I'm organizing."

Later, when the hurricane slammed water up the stairs to their walk-up, splitting the wood and making it groan, her mother's shoes would rise on top of the water like multicolored boats. Her mother's body would float on the water, too, but in a way much different from her shoes. Ten years later, that buoyancy still crept into Nichelle's dreams.

After the storm, she moved to L.A. The city never suited her, but her brother Stanley, the banker, had insisted that she come. He'd said she could help him and his wife, LeToya, with their toddler girls. LeToya was a lawyer. "And you can work and save money to get your own place," Stanley had said.

She worked at two fast-food restaurants. She rarely slept during these years and she never went out. Still, she saved enough to rent her own place, which was a dump, so she moved back to New Orleans to try again. But her home had changed. Faces of the dead were everywhere. So she moved back to L.A. She got a job with a home care agency and lived with Stanley again.

She wondered what her brother and his wife said about her when they were alone. Did they imagine she was happy to live this way, sleeping in their guest bedroom, braiding their daughters' hair and cooking their meals? Did they think she liked riding the bus to take care of old folks? Because she did not. And she sure as hell didn't want to be doing this for four more years until her nieces went off to college like their parents had, to places like Georgetown Law Center and Yale Business School.

Cathy said Nichelle worried too much. "Just live your life. You can't get caught up in what people think," she'd say.

Cathy lectured her one weekend as they walked the flea market looking for cloth. Nichelle planned to make scarves and hats for her nieces, for their school trip to the Alpine Meadows ski resort. "Don't act crazy about stuff," Cathy warned. When she said this, Nichelle stopped and rooted herself in the park dirt. She watched her friend pass the booth with silver jewelry and the Mexican Pinay food truck. When Cathy realized Nichelle was not beside her, she turned to look for her friend. "What?" Cathy said. She looked surprised.

"I'm not crazy and please don't suggest that I am."

"I'm just saying. Seems to me you get *really* worked up about things for no good reason. Your brother ain't asking you to leave, so just chill. Things are going to work out."

On Wednesday, before she went to Frank's, Nichelle rode the Metro to her therapist's office. She had five meetings to fulfill according to the court order. This Wednesday's meeting was her fourth. As she waited in the reception area, she distracted herself by pondering a crossword clue: "An island east of Corsica." Soon, she heard them call her name. She walked into an office decorated in beige and blue.

"How are things going?" Dr. Salas asked.

"Alright, I guess."

"Do you want to say more?"

"No, not really."

Dr. Salas moved a piece of candy around in her mouth. "Last week we talked about strategies to help you spend less time thinking about the past. Have you had success with that?"

"You mean the crosswords?"

"Are you doing crossword puzzles?"

"Yeah," Nichelle said. "It keeps my mind busy, you know."

She told Dr. Salas that things were okay except for the dreams. Her mother always appeared in these dreams to tell her what to do.

"Last night, I dreamt me and Stanley's family were skiing on a mountain and mama showed up saying, 'Why you acting like Stanley's third daughter?'"

In the dream, her mother wore a flowered dress and yellow sandals in the snow. She kept following Nichelle across the mountain and talking to her through increasing flurries. Nichelle remembered feeling cold and trying to follow what other people were doing on the hill.

"Like what? What were you trying to do?" Dr. Salas asked.

"I was trying to ski like everybody else."

"But you couldn't?"

"I could, but mama kept getting in the way and talking. She kept asking why I was still with Stanley and why was I trying to ski. She was confusing me. It was like, I couldn't concentrate when she talked—you know what I'm saying?"

Dr. Salas stared at Nichelle. The room filled with the smell of her mint candy.

"This is not really helping me, you know, talking to you like this," Nichelle said.

"What would you like for me to say?"

"I don't know. Something useful."

"Why do you think your mother keeps talking to you?"

Nichelle thought about this. "She's trying to help me get unstuck."

Dr. Salas leaned forward in her chair. "Why would she feel that you're stuck?"

"Because, look at me. I don't own nothing. I'm living with my little brother."

"But if your dream is trying to help you get unstuck, why worry about the details of *how* you're stuck?"

"Because those are constant reminders of my situation."

"Is it a reminder of why you're stuck or how you're stuck?"

Nichelle felt frustrated with this circular conversation. Thank god there was just one more of these sessions that she had to attend. "It's a reminder of *how* I'm stuck," she said.

Dr. Salas turned her head to gaze at a blue painting on her wall. "Okay, so we know *how* you're stuck. But you can't change your situation and dwell on how bad it is at the same time."

The bus ride from her therapist's office to Frank's neighborhood took twenty-five minutes. And the walk from the bus stop to Frank's took Nichelle straight past her gingerbread house. She liked the way sunlight broke over the roof's apex and fractured into small beams across the sidewalk and grass. She stayed across the street as she walked, careful not to violate the court's instructions.

When she reached Frank's street, he was in front of his bungalow watering his tomato plants. "Mr. Yee, I'm here. Ready for the barbershop?" she asked. Her first impression of Frank had been of him poking around the garden in a drawstring hat.

She hadn't even known that there were neighborhoods like Frank's in L.A., streets where people lived in houses for dozens of years, where they planted vegetables in their front yards and wore unfashionable straw hats. A trendy crowd was trickling in, but they were still much fewer in number than the old-timers like Frank Yee.

Frank had a broad face with deep creases that ran across it like smiles. On her first day of work, Nichelle had admired his face. He introduced her to his neighbor of twenty years who owned peacocks and had odd ways, and for the first time since living in L.A., Nichelle felt that she might stay. She imagined living in her own house in this very neighborhood. Auntie Shellie, as her nieces called her, would have a place all her own.

"I'm ready. Let's do this," Frank said. He turned off the water hose and went back to the porch to close and lock his door. He let Nichelle drive his car because he trusted her. She drove his Honda down Sunset, past billboards written in various languages, and past the brightly lit Quickie Mart where day laborers gathered outside in the parking lot. She pulled up to a barbershop in a shopping plaza with a clay-tiled roof.

Frank walked into the shop and sat in a chair. A young barber with tattoos that covered the length of his arms caped the old man. Nichelle took a seat in a chair against the wall. Her hands began to tremble in her lap. Thus began her day of driving around the city, watching Frank take care of his business, and making sure that he ate a good meal before she left. For today's supper, she would probably make some kind of fish. She pulled out her crossword book and glanced at her watch. She usually wrote her start time at the top of each puzzle, but she decided against her usual quirks on this day. She needed to stop with the weird rituals. That's how it started for her mother. First, she obsessed over organizing her shoes. Then, silverware. Next, her mother thought long and hard about colors. She became very particular about the arrangement of colored objects in their house. Toward the end, Nichelle would catch her mother mumbling words to herself, unaware.

"What are you talkin about?" she asked her mother one day.

"I was responding to a question my boss asked at work."

"But you not at work."

"I know," her mother said. "But you know how somebody says something to you and you don't have a good response at the time? And then you keep thinking about it and thinking about what you might have said?"

"I guess," Nichelle replied.

"That's all I was doing—saying to myself what I should have said to that bitch when I had the chance."

Instead of thinking about the start time for her puzzle, Nichelle decided simply to start.

Of course, working a crossword puzzle all day in her mind was no different than mumbling to herself. It was no different than revisiting past conversations and speaking them out loud to nobody. Puzzles were a way for Nichelle to distract herself from the horrors that would otherwise flood her mind. Like the memory of those evacuation buses that arrived after the storm.

The buses had smelled rotten. Nichelle had reluctantly climbed aboard. For her trip, she had no identification, no suitcase, and no personal belongings. She had only her social security number and name, which she repeated often, and which people sometimes wrote down, as if the name Nichelle Aubry would matter at some point to someone.

She got on the bus wearing the same clothes she'd had on for three days. She looked for a window seat. She found one in the middle, next to another woman who was cradling a young boy. As she climbed over the boy and woman to get to her seat, Nichelle held her arms down to her sides, and said, "Sorry, excuse me. I'm sorry." She was apologizing for her body's odor. She hadn't bathed since the storm and her period had started. Whenever she saw paper, she grabbed it and found a private place, preferably a bathroom, where she could stuff the paper into her soggy underwear to sop the blood.

Nichelle would not remember how long she sat on the bus without going anywhere, but at some point she would notice that it was growing dark outside and she was still on a parked bus in Orleans Parish. Two men and one woman would come on board and pass out food, which she ate. Then she fell asleep. When it was completely dark outside, the bus would pull out of its parked position and head west. Cool air would blow down from the ceiling, making her sneeze. She would rest with her head against the vibrating window. She would sleep overnight in shelters in Houston and Phoenix. Eventually, she would arrive in L.A.

"I want to go visit my wife," Frank said as they left the barbershop. He ran his hand through his newly cut hair. "How do I look?"

"You look good, Frank. I always tell you that. I'm hoping to look as good as you when I'm your age."

He laughed. Frank was so easy.

"What's that?" he asked her.

"What's what?" she said.

"You said, 'an island east of Corsica.'"

"I did?" Nichelle asked.

"Yes you did," Frank replied.

She laughed.

"You know how you think of something from earlier and you just keep working it out in your mind? That's what I was doing. But I've got to stop mumbling to myself. Thanks for pointing it out," she said.

They got inside his car and drove off. Frank slid money out of his billfold. "What's this one?" Frank asked Nichelle. He held the bill away from his face. He squinted and flipped it back and forth.

"That's a twenty. They're all twenties, except for this one. That's a ten. And you've got two fives. All twenties, a ten and two fives," she said.

"Enough for flowers and groceries?"

"I think so," Nichelle said.

She drove north on La Brea. When she crossed Wilshire, Frank turned and pointed to a store. "Pull over here," he said.

Nichelle looked into the rearview mirror at the cars behind them. "You have to give me more time than that," she said. She drove past the flower shop where Frank wanted to go. She circled back through a neighborhood of fancy one-way streets. She went at least fifteen minutes out of her way to get back to the store.

"No easy way to get around this city," she said. "Not like at home."

Inside the flower shop, Frank picked up a bouquet with stalks of white gladiolas, pink tiger lilies, and red roses. "What's the sign say for these?" he asked.

Nichelle bent down to read the sign. "$24.99 for those. They're pretty, Frank. I think your wife will like them," she said.

They talked about Frank's wife as if she were alive. That's what Frank pre-ferred even though his wife was as dead as Nichelle's mother. But he said things to Nichelle like, "What do you think my wife wants me to bring when I visit her today?" She was buried in an L.A. cemetery. The one with the big rolling hills.

When they arrived at the cemetery, Nichelle helped Frank from the car. She held onto his arm as they walked up the biggest hill. When they reached his wife's grave in the northeast corner, she left Frank there. She walked back down the hill. She watched different people visit grave sites. One woman, a nurse, was dressed in purple scrubs. The woman kept wiping her face with a tissue that was crumbling apart.

Months before, LeToya had suggested nursing as a possible career for Nichelle.

Nichelle had just arrived home from work. She had been excited to talk to LeToya about a house that she'd seen for sale. Her sister-in-law was in the living room. She was in trial at the time, court documents spread across the living room floor. She was drinking coffee to stay alert. She nervously fingered the twists in her hair.

Nichelle dropped her duffle onto the floor. "I think I've found a place to live," she said.

"Where?"

"It's near Frank in Echo Park."

"Echo Park?" LeToya asked.

"Yes."

"Oh, Shellie," LeToya said, "that will be too expensive for you."

Nichelle ignored her. "Look at the pictures," she said. She showed her sister-in-law photos of the Victorian that she'd taken on her phone. There were at least a dozen pictures taken from several angles and various distances.

"It's gorgeous," LeToya said. "You can call the realtor, but Sis, property has become expensive over there. You see where we live, and Stan and I both have good jobs."

There was an awkward silence after that comment. During the pause, Nichelle looked at her phone and flipped through more photos of the house.

"You should think of going to nursing school like we talked about," Le-Toya continued. "Even then, you might not earn enough for a place like that, but you'd have more money at least. It takes a lot of money," she said.

Nichelle hated that LeToya was right. Weeks after their conversation, her dream house sold for half a million dollars. When the new owners moved in, Nichelle tried to break herself from what had become her daily routine. Each day, she had walked by that house. Sometimes she stopped and took several pictures. Each day she had planned an elaborate future for herself that involved living in that home. It had become such a fixed idea that Nichelle could not let it go.

At the grocery store, she pointed to vegetables and fruit and asked Frank what he wanted to purchase.

"Apples?"

"No. Too hard to bite."

"Bananas?" she asked.

"Maybe, but just a few."

Like most older people, Frank didn't eat much. He liked cereal in the morning and he ate something small later in the day. Tonight, it would be trout and potatoes. They left the store with two paper bags and returned to Frank's bungalow.

As she drove through the neighborhood, she passed the Victorian once again. She glanced at the olive tree out front. Because winter had been mild this year, the olives had come in early. She could see the dark fruit in the branches. She did not mention olives to Frank. She knew he couldn't see them from this distance.

Plus, she was embarrassed by her obsession with this place. She was supposed to forget the house. To not look. To do something else. The court had ordered Nichelle not to come within 100 feet of the house. There had been a whole ridiculous proceeding inside a courthouse, where she had to wear good clothes and swear to tell the truth on a bible. Her brother Stanley's testimony had been the only bright spot during the proceeding. He testified that Nichelle was a loving person and a hard worker but said she'd suffered many misfortunes. She'd laughed inappropriately at that because she thought, *Who doesn't have misfortunes?* The judge instructed her not to laugh.

"She deserves another chance," Stanley had said for the record. "I see my big sister rising above this. She's right there, your Honor. She's at a point where she's getting her life together. She's decided to make Los Angeles her home, and with a little help, she's getting ready to turn it around and move up at work and in life. I can see it. I know her. I've been knowing her all of my life. I know that she's resilient." When he said the last part, he looked Nichelle in the eyes. "And maybe my wife and I can do more to help her out."

"Well, it seems to the court that you've done quite a bit already," the judge said. He turned in his high chair to face her. He asked Nichelle why she had broken the window and whether she felt any remorse. Nichelle was silent.

"Ms. Aubry?" the judge said.

"Yes?"

"Did you hear my questions to you?"

"Yes."

"Would you answer them, please."

"I didn't mean to break the window. I'm sorry for that," Nichelle said. "And I apologize if I scared anyone. But I won't apologize for expressing how I felt at that moment."

"Exactly what were you expressing, Ms. Aubry?"

Nichelle looked at Stanley and LeToya sitting there in the front row. Although LeToya practiced in federal court, and they were in state court now, this was her sister-in-law's professional community and Nichelle felt ashamed to have done this to her. She'd dragged their family's business into the courts, sullying her sister-in-law's good name. "I don't know. I was feeling—" She started but didn't finish her sentence.

Nichelle knew what everyone thought about her, and maybe what she thought about herself. That she needed to take better advantage of the opportunities given to her. She needed to be "personally responsible." That's what her therapist wrote down in her file. "Work on individual responsibility." "Ownership of problems." That's what Dr. Salas thought, and what they all thought. They believed that Nichelle needed to work a little harder, to focus herself on her goals. After the hurricane, she had been given unemployment benefits and other compensation and, yes, she was making more money now than she did before the disaster, but it still wasn't nearly enough. It wasn't ever enough. And she couldn't help but feel that something in her life wasn't fair. That she didn't have a fighting chance. She saw that. All this talk that people did to her as if she needed a lesson to inspire her toward greatness was bullshit in her mind. She'd never have that house, or any house, and the thought of that made her want to throw her head back in the courtroom and howl like a goddamned wolf. The idea of howling like a wolf made her laugh.

"Ms. Aubry, I'm not going to tell you again. Please stop laughing," the judge said.

She was not sorry for looking in that house, for wanting that house. At least she would have one witness to the deep ache that she carried in her gut.

Around four o'clock, Nichelle cooked Frank's dinner and placed a plate of warm food on his table. Next Wednesday she would be done with this legal bullshit and could move forward or backward, or whatever. She sat opposite Frank and opened her crossword book. She wanted to count how many puzzles she had left to solve, but she resisted the urge. *No compulsive stuff, not tonight.* She'd focus on the puzzle at hand.

"What's an island east of Corsica?" she asked Frank. He sat there for a moment, thinking. In the window behind him, pink light hovered at the horizon.

"Sardinia?" Frank said.

She counted. "Too many letters."

"Taipei?"

"Nope."

She saw that Frank was fumbling with his silverware. Perhaps his eyes were foggier than she had thought. She moved her chair beside him and picked up his fork and knife. She cut the food into bite-sized chunks as he sat there and watched her slice into the potatoes and fish. She could not know exactly what he saw, but *she* was looking at food that she had prepared for a man with no family left. That lifted her spirits some. She noticed the flakes of white meat floating in sauce and the tender red skin that was separating from her boiled potatoes. She scooped some of the stew onto Frank's fork using her fingers. Frank closed his eyes and opened his mouth. Her hand shook, but she raised the fork and she fed him. She fed him without dropping his food.

Who Do You Love?

I first saw Priscilla at the pawnshop as the Arizona sun reddened the sky at dusk. It was just before closing. She looked Jamaican to me, but maybe I was homesick. Still, something was familiar about her—the gapped teeth, the regal posture, the locked hair she'd tied in an upsweep that resembled a bird's nest. Honorable is how she struck me, unlike our usual female customers with the belly out and the low-rise jeans that show the top of their underwear; underwear that ain't even *real*, mind you, but the G-strings chicks wear these days. When I first come to the States, only erotic dancers wore that sort of thing. Today, even the college girls that I've dated wear panty strings.

But Priscilla's skirt come to her knees. Her blouse was modest, a button-down loose-fitting deal, which you never see on women today. That let me know it was not brand new. So I think, maybe her money is a little tight, maybe she spends her money on drugs. Carney, the shop owner, says this about many of our customers.

See the one with the dirty hair? he'll say, leaning in close. She's a tweaker. She's here getting money to buy crystal meth.

He says that Phoenix has a huge meth problem, that everyone uses it. He read that in the newspaper. So now he judges them that come in and look like they might use. But he doesn't really know. And the truth is this: drug addicts are damned good for his pawnshop business.

What can I do for you? I asked her. The other employees had all gone. She looked in my eyes trying to appear unafraid, but *her* eyes were soft, which I liked.

I'm interested in selling some jewelry, she said.

Let me see what you have, I told her.

Carney was counting money behind the darkened glass. It was almost time to go home.

She pulled out a zipper sandwich bag and inside of it were two rings made of white gold. One was a simple band made for a man, and the other one was a woman's ring with a clear, round diamond. She watched me as I turned the gold circles between my fingers. I could feel her tremble inside, deep down where she thought nobody could see. It's all a performance, you understand. I pretend to assess the value, and the customer, if she's wise, will begin to talk up the value by telling me the jewelry is an heirloom or whatnot. None of this matters. What matters is whether we'll get more money from a loan or from resale. This requires a quick reading of the customer. I could tell that Priscilla would sell at a low price.

I pretended to note imperfections in the diamond, but I didn't use the jeweler's loupe because that seems over the top to me. I mean, come on, I'm not a jeweler; I don't look like one. From some customers, I get, *Dude, you look like Ziggy Marley*, because of my dreads and rusty complexion—a comment I hate—but I could never pass for a diamond expert, you see. Besides, I'm nearsighted, and to use the loupe you must remove your glasses, and I can't see a thing without them. Carney's got bad eyes too, but he says he's getting laser surgery. He'll do anything to make the girls think he is young.

I asked her to wait while I went in the back. You gotta see these rings, man, I said.

Carney peered at Priscilla through the one-way glass. Just offer her two and let's go, he said with his typical bluster. But before I could do that, he brushed past me and walked to the counter in the store. He looked at the rings. He cleaned the diamond, measured it, weighed it. I can loan you four-fifty, he said. Priscilla laughed. She had a sensuous mouth. It was wide and her gapped teeth hung slightly over a full bottom lip.

I have appraisal papers, she said. They say the diamond ring is worth thirty-four hundred dollars and the other ring is worth five hundred. She pulled out squares of paper and held them in her hand.

Yeah, those are inflated figures, Carney said, appraisers do that shit all the time.

She was silent because she was not a dealmaker, you understand. She knew that she needed to negotiate, but she didn't know how to do it. I have a sick child. I don't have time for this, she said. She began stuffing the valuation papers back into her purse.

Carney sighed. Are you looking for a loan or to sell?

I don't know. What's the difference?

Seven-fifty to sell. Four-fifty for a loan.

Okay, she said, let's do a sale.

Carney walked to the back office.

What's wrong with your child? I asked.

She smirked. There's always something with him, she said.

The thing about this business is I see all kinds of people. Musicians. Students. Addicts. Housewives. I try to put a story to each customer. What made them come in? Why are they pawning a camera? Sometimes I wonder if it's even *their* camera but I don't ask questions because the law does not require it unless I know the object is stolen. So I just do my job each day but in my head, you know, I'm trying to figure out what has happened and why this person needs a loan at this time.

I've shared some of these stories with Tran. When I first met Priscilla, Tran lived in the 400-square-foot apartment above mine with her husband and seven-year-old son. They were immigrants like me, looked Hakka Chinese, but instead of migrating from Kingston they had moved here from Hanoi. They'd been here fewer years than me, so I helped them with questions they had about American customs. That's how I met Tran. The manager had just shown her family the apartment and had given them a contract to sign.

I was coming in with groceries when Tran walked straight up in my face.

Please explain.

Excuse me? I said.

Please explain. Explain, she said, about the legal jargon that was in their rental agreement.

Tran visited when she was off work, I was off work, and her husband was at work, which wasn't often because we all worked most of each day. Tran worked at a bakery in the Willo district and a nail salon on 16th and Indian School. Back then, I worked for Carney during the week, and on weekends I bartended at a restaurant in the Biltmore Hotel. I had a few other hustles, too, nothing I liked to admit to or that I believed I'd be doing forever, but I was swindled by a business partner when I first come here and I was struggling, you know, to get back on my feet.

You know what I was thinking, Trevor? Tran says to me one day. I have nothing I can pawn. If I needed money right away, I have nothing I can pawn.

You could sell the drum set, I said. Her boy's Rockwood Jr. sprawled in the front room of their apartment. It took up more space than their furniture.

He would cry, she said.

You could sell the DVDs.

Tran's husband collected movies. They were mostly gangster flicks, but he also owned bootlegged karate movies, and the 1978 version of *Dawn of the Dead*.

How much I get for them? she asked.

Forty, maybe fifty bucks.

That's all? Tran said, That's not enough.

And this is true; we never give a customer what she hopes to receive. I see it all the time. The disappointment and compromise. The questions about what one is owed, what to keep, and what one can part with forever.

The deal with Priscilla, I guessed, was that her old man was away, that he'd hit bricks, or maybe dude died, but in any case she was left to sell the one thing of value that she owned—their wedding rings. Probably thought she'd never part with them, that they would be wearing them on the Judgment Day. That's why she appeared contrite that night in the shop because that is what a hard decision does, it humbles you. I remember how she'd confessed her innocence to us, *I don't know. What's the difference?* she'd asked, and we'd taken advantage of her anyway, selling the rings for eighteen hundred dollars two weeks after her visit. First rule in this business is never show vulnerability. I wish she'd known that. These rocker kids—the ones with gauges and tattoos, addict pimples all over their face—they bluff a macho stance for cash all day long. They make me sick. Then along comes a woman who offers rings during a difficult time, and she is so open about what she needs that it shook me up.

●

She returned in the fall when the weather was cooler and such. She wore a shapeless dress that day, but it failed to hide the thickness of her ass. Her hair was down, which flattered her face, and I could see the occasional gray hair tangled in a few of her dreads.

I was helping some joker who was trying to pawn fake Rolex watches. Brother, these have no resale value, I told him, then I made my way down the jewelry counter to her.

There are some women, like the young girls I serve at the bar, who are fully aware of their power. Their faces are made up like peacock feathers and with every twitch of their barely-covered bodies, they entice the men who are always watching. These girls are fun to talk to. Then there are women like Priscilla, whom many in the States seem not to see. Priscilla enchanted me through practiced understatement.

Didn't expect to see you back in here, I said.

I need to sell a guitar.

She showed me an acoustic Fender that was pretty in a slick, mass-produced sort of way.

You play? I asked.

Not anymore, a little bit in college.

Can I ask where you're from?

She raised her eyebrows to let me know that I'd invaded her privacy. I shrugged as apology. I thought maybe you were Jamaican, I said. You look like the women I knew in Kingston.

Are you flirting with me? she asked, because I suspect I'm not your usual type.

I laughed. Anyway, I said, we can give you twenty dollars for the guitar. You could get more from Zucker's Guitars on Third. You should check with them, let me know if you get a better offer.

I wrote the store's address on a slip of paper. Out of the corner of my eye I saw Carney making his way over to where we were, to make sure that I wasn't stealing. He is paranoid that way. He thinks we want to steal money from him all the time, that we cut deals with the customers and take money off the top or that we have fences for friends and we direct his customers to them. Carney has a biker friend who wears his sideburns cut into crazy designs and Carney brings this guy in as a scare tactic when he thinks somebody is stealing. The guy can't find reason to get in my face but that don't stop Carney from keeping an eye on me if I talk to a customer for too long.

I slid the address across the glass counter to show Carney that I had nothing to hide. I am smarter than him. I've learned to be smarter since the swindling.

Your kid better? I asked Priscilla.

Sort of. We were in urgent care the other night, she said.

Carney walked up to us wearing this disco shirt, his attempt to be a retro hipster.

Everything cool here? he asked.

We're cool, boss man, I snarked.

At the end of the evening, only me and this kid, Skee, were left. Skee was new and Carney made him do shit work like dust the display merchandise and kill scorpions. Carney had locked the doors, and he and I were counting money in the showroom so that he could keep an eye on Skee.

While Carney watched Skee, I was skimming money from my pile. Just a little bit, you know, to help me with my bills. I'd slide every other ten from my right thumb back to the pile in my left hand. It was our least common bill. When Carney was distracted, I'd ball it and drop it on the floor. Then I'd step on it with my foot, let Carney get up from the table first. It was simple and I did it quick-like. It helped that Carney was damn near blind.

Trevor, he said as we counted, who was the chick with the guitar?

She was here this summer, I said, with the wedding bands. Remember?

I know *that*. Why was she back in here?

I don't know boss man. Because she needs money?

You know what, Trevor?

What?

You're a dick.

You know what, Carney? I said, but he was silent. You should grow one.

Skee moved around in his skinny-legged jeans trying to stay above our poppy show.

I don't trust her.

I laughed. Like you trust anybody, I said.

At a quarter to eleven, we pulled the iron gates over the doors and windows, and set the alarm. Carney was weird about who could stay at closing because he didn't want everyone to know how the security system worked. I heard talk that the place had been robbed years ago when his father was the owner and that Carney had not been the same since then. Skee stood around biting his nails as Carney and I turned off lights and got the place right. When we finished, Carney let us out through the back door.

I unchained my bike and started the ride home. I like bike riding during the cool months because I get to see the desert close up in a way that I never do when riding the bus. Besides, it saves me bus fare for about seven months of the year. In central Phoenix, the avenues and neighborhoods are cramped and flat, but there are fields near the mountains that are undeveloped, where the earth becomes hilly and the dust and gravel crunches under your wheels as you pedal along. There aren't any real paths, only areas where the sagebrush or cactus don't grow, and that's where I ride, following the open spaces between the low-lying shrubs, the mountains dark and silent all around.

I could see light coming from Tran's apartment. She'd taken the shade off the lamp again, and from outside, the window framed a ball of white light that was muted by gauzy drapes she'd hung in the window. I locked my bike and climbed the stairs two at a time. My place was a mess inside. I'd forgotten to wash the dishes and the smell of dried spaghetti sauce was thick in the air.

I grabbed a beer and flopped onto the sofa. There were footsteps above me and muffled sounds from Tran's television. She agreed that we needed to stop seeing each other before shit got scary. Still, it was weird hearing her move around and not being able to see her or to smell the citrus oil that she wore.

She'd come by the first of October and we'd shared coffee and cigarettes together, trying to be friends. She loved her husband—I knew that—and honestly, I didn't like sneaking around, especially with her kid and all because he was intelligent, you know, you could see it in his eyes, and who knows what he thought about me, what he saw when he looked at me, or what he would remember about me and his mom when he became a big boy and some random memory came floating up and caught him unaware.

Priscilla returned to the shop in late November. Zucker's had given her a better deal for her guitar and she came by to thank me for the tip.

I'm not going to stay long because Jamal is waiting outside, she said.

Your boy? Where he at? I asked.

She pointed. Through the window I could see her son leaning on an old Toyota. He had that lanky, fourteen-year-old look. He hadn't grown into his lips or feet yet, and his baggy shorts exposed his twiggy shins.

I'd imagined her son to be little, maybe because she'd spoken of him like he was defenseless, but he was clearly a teenager and he was listening to music, reciting words the way kids do, his snapback perched at a cocky angle.

He looked normal from a distance.

You like coffee?

You offering? she asked. She was smiling. When is the last time you dated an African *American* woman?

I leaned on the jewelry counter. A couple years back, I said.

Two years?

Maybe four or five.

Oh, I see, she said.

I stood upright. Only because I work all the time, I said. I bartend at the Biltmore and not a lot of sisters come in there, you know.

You bartend? So you can make cocktails, but you're offering me coffee?

We both laughed.

I'm not going to make you coffee, I said. I'd like to buy you a cup of coffee, you know, when you have the time.

Priscilla was a records clerk at Banner Health. I liked the way her tongue looked through her gap when she said the *l*'s in her name. We linked up at a coffee shop one afternoon. The following week, we walked for hours through a shopping mall. I was embarrassed that our dates were so low budget but she didn't seem to mind. She wasn't a fussy girl, which I'd already known.

Priscilla and Jamal lived near South Mountain in a house on a weedy lot. Jamal's dad had been the sort who came and left as he pleased, but the previous year Priscilla had told him not to return. She had no idea where he was now. There was evidence of his time in the house: a couple of fist-sized holes in the wall.

Her boy had a limp that was caused by one leg being shorter than the other. Priscilla said the leg was a congenital disorder but doctors weren't sure about other symptoms that he had. They were thinking food allergies, now. She could talk endlessly about his battles with digestion, headaches, and common colds, and how he struggled to be a normal kid. One night, awakened by noise, I found her in the bathroom double-checking Jamal's medicines and prescriptions. Vials and bottles covered the bathroom counter.

Her hands shook as she moved the bottles across the counter. Sweat was on her brow and a small drop of mucous was creeping from one of her nostrils.

I have to make sure he has all of his doses for tomorrow. If he misses just one, it could be a bad day, she said. She wiped her nose with the back of her hand.

I loved how fiercely she protected Jamal. She'd found the nerve to walk into Carney's pawnshop in order to provide for him. I'd met Carney during my bad years, too. I knew the courage that it took to sell your personal possessions, to sell rings just so you can eat.

When the holidays ended, the pawnshop entered a sales slump. To keep busy, Carney made Skee go around spraying glass cleaner on the jewelry counters and store windows, but mostly we just hung out and talked a lot of shit.

It began to rain for days in a row and plants were blooming in tiny bursts of color. As I'd ride through town, I'd see yellow shoots from the Agave, and the tight red buds of the Joshua Tree. Rainwater collected in fields, creating muddy pools of water that I tried to dodge. Sometimes I'd hit these puddles head on; I wouldn't see them because my glasses were fogged from the weather. When I'd get home, I'd have to spray my bike with a hose to remove the red dirt. I'd wash the bike, take a shower, and then I'd go out again to meet up with Priscilla.

I was spending a lot of time with her, so I didn't notice the messages on my cell phone at first. I had two voicemails that were a day old when I finally listened to them. The woman's voice was pleasant despite the official tone, and her name, Marisel, I liked. She was a social worker with the State of Arizona, she said. I'm calling to talk to you about Jamal.

I listened to the messages as rain fell outside in a steady drizzle. I could hear Tran's boy practicing a swing pattern on his drums, which meant that his old man—who hated the noise—wasn't there. Soon, Tran was at my door to borrow cigarettes. Her hair looked like she'd just washed and blown it dry. A breeze blew onto the balcony and fanned her hair around her face.

Sorry, I'm out, I said. I stood in the doorway so as not to invite her in.

That's not like you to run out of cigarettes, Tran said.

She bit her lip while I stood there. I said nothing. I let her remark dangle.

Sometimes a customer at a bar gets drunk enough to tell me his story. What he says is not true. In fact, it is always bullshit, because drunkenness does not inspire honesty but bravado. And so the insurance adjuster becomes a corporate executive or the music teacher brags about playing at The House of Blues, which may be true, but the story of who they really are, of how they struggle to pay their phone bill, gets left out of the storytelling.

One time a guy come into the Biltmore bar saying that he knew who shot Biggie Smalls, and he was dressed like a rapper, you know, had large diamonds in his ears and the platinum and such and this is a bar where mostly professionals hang out after leaving the office, so they were awed that this guy could buy several rounds of drinks and they listened to him and asked him questions and he left the bar with a woman who had silicone tits.

What I see in Priscilla is the opposite of all that. I don't care what others like Marisel may think of her. Marisel, who thinks Priscilla is making her own boy sick. I see how adversity has made Priscilla more authentic, more beautiful and soldier-like. It has warped her, too, as it has me, but no one makes it through life without some harm.

I spoke to Marisel early one morning.

How'd you get my number? I asked

Priscilla gave it to me. She didn't tell you?

She may have told me, I said, and I forgot.

You won't mind giving me a minute of your time then? I just have routine questions about Jamal's wellness.

I didn't respond, but Marisel jumped right in. Can you describe Jamal's mood lately? she asked.

Pretty happy.

And you base that on?

The usual stuff. His mom does right by him.

Upstairs I could hear Tran's family making their morning sounds. Running water. Television. Clink of dishes. Tran and her husband were arguing in Vietnamese, a language that I don't understand.

And his health?

What about it?

From what you've observed, any protracted illnesses, maybe missing school a lot?

Maybe a day here and there. He does have the leg thing, you know.

Would you consider his mother's concern appropriate at these times?

It was a good question. What's appropriate between mother and son? Or when you've been betrayed by people you trusted? Yes, I said, there's nothing Priscilla wouldn't do for her son. We ended our conversation after that.

I suppose I could have become worried about the phone call or what I could imagine was in Jamal's file. Imagination is like that, you know. You can take an ordinary person and situation and turn them monstrous in your mind. Instead, I sat and watched the rain, which comes during one season if it comes at all.

The next day I took Priscilla and Jamal to the racetrack near Gila River Casino. The sun was out. You could see the snow-capped mountains and it was one of those days when the desert feels like a blessing. We watched the cars race around piled tires, the sun beaming down on their neon-colored frames, the engines sounding like a swarm of bees.

Jamal climbed the spectator stand swinging his short leg. He looked like an old man. He was headed to the top but Priscilla didn't want him to climb that high.

What's wrong with watching from here? she asked him.

'Cause I don't wanna sit that close.

I don't think you should climb all the way up there.

I'm alright.

You'll be talking about your leg bothering you.

Mama!

He'll be okay, I said.

There weren't many people who showed up, maybe thirty in all. They were relatives of the amateur racers or people like us who had little else to do on a Sunday morning. Most of us sat in the middle of the stands, but Jamal stayed at the top, listening to his music. After a while, a couple of boys joined him. I could see them, when I glanced over my shoulder, sharing their headphones and talking smack the way young boys will do.

Who is he talking to? Priscilla asked at one point.

I pulled her hand to my mouth and gave it a playful bite.

Ow, Trevor! That hurts.

The boy's alright, I said. Give him some space.

You give me some space. Why are you judging how I parent? What if I were critical of things that you do?

She twisted, trying to free herself from my grip, but I held tight to her wrist. I didn't know it then, but I would stay with Priscilla. I would change jobs to make more money. I'd drop my hustles and help her raise up the boy.

Later, Tran came by to return a borrowed cooking pot. In my kitchen, she told me that her husband had confronted her about our affair.

We're moving because of it, she said.

When?

At the end of the month. Shame was all over her face.

I went to stand next to her. I threw my arm across her shoulders and squeezed her into my side. She dropped her head against my chest. I wanted to say something that would redeem what we'd done, but the words never came. We just stood there on my gray, tiled floor. After she left, the smell of citrus oil lingered so I started to clean the apartment. I wiped counters, washed clothes, swept, and polished. I sorted through piles of interim junk I'd been hoarding for too many years.

You Can Kiss All of That Bye-Bye

These days, I'm inclined to think that my eccentric parents are going insane. I consider flying back home to see if this is true because these things are hard to gauge via video chat. They look crazy when we talk. Perhaps they are displaying the first signs of dementia, but how can I be sure? Last week, as my mother goes on and on about some cooking show that she likes to watch, my father thrusts his face across my computer screen. Babygirl, he says, Your mother is controlling my thoughts through her food. When you come home, you're going to find a zombified version of me and don't say that I didn't warn you. Afterwards, my mother adjusts the camera onto her face and resumes talking about shrimp frittata.

Dad, can you stop it? I say before mother wrestles the computer away. I'm trying to stretch my leg as I talk to my folks. A million frustrations are ahead of me: An appointment with an arthroscopic surgeon, dance rehearsals, the jeans I cannot wriggle into without sharp pain shooting through my knee. I stare into my computer looking for signs that my parents are okay. You know that's a harmful archetype don't you? This idea of a conjure woman who casts an evil spell?

Exactly, my mother says. She is proud that I recognize historical representations and misrepresentations of womanhood. Her scholarship, years ago, was in the emerging field of women's studies. Her big regret is that she did not contribute more to this discipline, but who in the end will blame her? The jobs she got barely paid her bills, when here comes my father, an R&B singer, who promises to take care of her needs. She was first-generation Bahamian in the U.S. She was here on a visa that would soon expire.

My parents married and moved to a rambler in Oakland County, Michigan, where, my mom has told me, she thought she would eventually pick up and finish her dissertation. All these years later, she's still ABD. But the power of ideas animates her every move. I've caught her mumbling her thoughts as she cleans glass tabletops with vinegar and newspaper, as she flips conch fritters in their popping oil.

She is an especially astute reader of other people. Your father is the type that loves to be in charge, she told me when I was nine. It burns him up that he was just a back-up singer, you know. That's why he pushes you so. We were in the gymnasium for my school's production of *The Sound of Music*, and I had just left the stage after the first act, in tears. During the performance, students in the audience had mocked my portrayal of Maria, and they'd laughed out loud at the kiss I performed with Kevin Susser, who played Captain von Trapp.

I'm not going back out there, I announced. I don't know what I expected my parents to do with that. Perhaps I thought they would kiss the top of my carefully braided head or offer some gesture to demonstrate their solidarity with my childhood suffering. That's what Mike and Carol Brady did each week on *The Brady Bunch*. At the time, my favorite episode was the one in which Bobby plots to run away. When his mother hears of this, she packs her own suitcase and declares that she will follow Bobby wherever he goes. The episode ends once Bobby understands that he is loved.

To say that my father was unlike Mr. and Mrs. Brady would fail to capture the full flavor of his sadistic style of parenting. When I refused to go back onstage, my father grabbed the soft meat on the back of my neck. He pinched it. You want to be ordinary, huh? Or extraordinary? He asked me this with his face in my face. A trickle of sweat made its way out of his right sideburn. I remember blinking my eyes, trying to make sense of his abstract words.

I knew that extraordinary was a higher goal than ordinary, but what did extraordinary look like? Wasn't heckling from the audience evidence that I was not only ordinary but perhaps a terrible actress? You are a great performer, my father said, as if he could read my mind. Go out there and throw your heart into the second act if you don't want a whooping when we get home. Moments before the second act, as I prepared to walk onstage, he said, Remember! Throw your heart into it. Do it until their clapping sounds like love.

I guess my father is thinking of his own advice these days because he's returning to music even though he is in his seventies. Over the years, he has figured out ways to stay in the public eye through speaking engagements and writing a memoir, but this time he intends to record new songs. Really? I say, studying his face on my computer screen. But he talks as if things have been set in motion as we speak. He says he has hired an agent. And your mother is fighting me like she fights me on everything, he says. She's trying to control my thoughts through stuff that she's putting in my food. Oh, Daddy, I say, but he insists, She is. This talk of mind control seems a little extra, even for him, so my partner Mike and I discuss what's going on and I purchase a roundtrip ticket to Detroit.

It's late October when I arrive, and the sight of vermillion trees tugs at my throat. I feel a certain nostalgia for home. That feeling completely leaves by the first night. My father is right: my mother's compulsive cooking resembles some sort of deep-seated mania. It's not the dark arts or mind control as he suggests, but the volume of her cooking and preoccupation with cooking is weird. This is the never-ending story with my folks. They use their eccentricities to mess with each other. Your mum's a bit screwy, Mike said after the first time he met my parents. And she picks on your dad, likes to boss him around. What are you talking about? I replied. My mother gave up her research to support his career. That's not picking on him, that's called having his back.

This is not to say that I regard my mom as innocent. The first thing I notice when I arrive home is all of her canning supplies pushed up against one wall. Boxes of food processors balance one on top of the other against a second wall. Why she needs more than one food processor or a year's supply of canned food, I do not know. Then there are the vegetable roots, perhaps potatoes, growing in jars placed on counters and in the windows. Dried herbs are piled in heaps. In the kitchen, a stock pot bubbles with gelatinous froth.

As I peer into each room, I understand my father's complaints. No, he is not being mind-controlled, but my mother has overwhelmed the space with an unbelievable amount of foodstuff. It stretches from the kitchen to the dining room, bedrooms, and den. Cookbooks are stacked on end tables collecting dust, or maybe that's flour. This place is a mess, I say, as I hobble around on my bum knee. Clearly, my parents have lost interest in maintaining their home and that's fine. But the cooking, Good Lord, I've never seen so much of it. Everything in the house is an object of my mother's obsession. When I was a girl, things felt exactly opposite. The home I remember showed off my father's accomplishments. His awards and photographs covered the walls and curio cabinets. If those trophies and pictures are still around, they have been tucked into corners of the crawl space or cedar closet where they remain out of sight.

In my mind, the easiest way to deal with my parents' situation is to sell the rambler and move them into an assisted living facility. That way they can meet other retirees and attend scheduled events. They could be busy and avoid this odd behavior, which I want to attribute to their fear of growing old. I mention the idea of assisted living on Day Four at breakfast. My father says, Babygirl, please. We're not doing that. My mother just does that thing with her lips that translates roughly into "whatever." We're sitting at a round table on which my mother has placed scrambled eggs, lemon bars, fried potatoes, and fruit salad sprinkled with sprigs of fresh mint. There's also leftover steak, chow mein, and pan-fried kielbasa, because who doesn't want a little Chinese carryout and hot dogs with their breakfast at nine a.m.? Daddy refuses to taste any of it. With a trembling hand, he has poured his own coffee that he made in a pot separate from the one that mother and I share.

Well, I tell them, if you won't consider selling the house, I insist that you take a long vacation. Come and visit me and Mike for a few months in Seattle.

You sure you want us there? my mother says. You and Michael are so private. What do you do anyway? Do you even go out?

I don't begrudge my mother for speaking this truth. Mike and I have built a quiet, almost monastic life in an apartment near Puget Sound. We choreograph at our theater company, do a couple of shows each year, but otherwise we stay to ourselves. It costs money to leave the apartment, and we don't have much of it. Every now and then we host a dinner party for our friends, Leah and Gordon.

Is the theater company in the black? my father asks.

No, I say, but our last show was nominated for a Drama League Award.

I think you told us that, daddy says before changing the subject. He mentions his plans to meet with record executives sometime next spring in Los Angeles. These are meetings that his new agent has scheduled.

Have you met the agent? I ask my mother.

I have not, she says.

Of course you haven't, my father says, because she lives in L.A.

I don't doubt my father's ability to court good luck. He grew up a poor boy in eastern Kentucky and became a famous singer who traveled the world. When he first talked of publishing a memoir, mother and I thought it a fanciful idea since we had never seen him write more than one page of prose. But he wrote an entire book without a ghostwriter, without anyone's help. You get a limited number of opportunities in life, he likes to say, and I wonder what he must think about mine. I muddle through each year. I dropped out of college. I've been rejected at an embarrassing number of dance auditions. I fell in love with a Brit-Canadian who convinced me to sink my money into a theater company that we can barely manage. And now, at thirty-seven, I have a knee injury that could end my not-so-successful career.

At these failures I feel sadness and sometimes shame. After our Drama League nomination, Mike and I flew out to New York for the awards ceremony. This is it, we thought, this will be our big break. And then we lost. The nomination helped when we applied for grants for our theater company. We produced a few more shows because of it, but even I was surprised at how quickly it became another line on our resumes, a missed chance, an almost-made-it type of thing.

Maybe we'll stop in Seattle when I go to L.A. in March, my father says.

I don't want a hurried stopover on your way to California. I want you and mom to stay for a few months, to get out of this struggle being waged inside of the home. My mother sucks her teeth as if I'm talking complete nonsense. I didn't raise you up to be a dutiful woman, she says as she pushes daddy's cup from the table's edge.

If they had been other parents, I might have ended up with a different life. Maybe I would have married, had children, bought a house in a neighborhood fifty miles or so from where I grew up. But I had Richmond "Ricky" Roberts and Igrid Braithwaite as my parents. I heard rumors growing up that my mother wasn't my real mother, that my real mother had been a groupie who slept with my dad. I spent entire summers in places like Ibiza, Spain, in a hotel room with other children of Motown singers and musicians. I watched one kid get his fat head stuck between the railings of our hotel balcony. I saw famous people get high and overdose. And I watched my mother's face through the years, the way her mouth pulled down at the corners when she smoked her cigarettes, as if everything she tasted and saw in life was sour. Years ago, when I told my mother that I was thinking about having children, she startled to attention. Why would you do that? she asked. You can't travel or do anything with kids. I reminded her that we traveled to many places as a family, but she insisted that was a different era and situation. You need to focus on yourself, she said. As if she had ever done the same.

On Day Eight, I'm in the kitchen, where mom is baking an applesauce cake that she dusts with powdered sugar. Because it's your favorite, she says to my dad. Says who? he responds. I don't want your cake. After a loud argument about what he will and will not do, he gives in to her request to eat one slice.

For the first time since I've been home, a sense of peace settles in. In that moment, it feels as if we are trying to be a normal family, we've abandoned the idiosyncrasies. The three of us sit beneath the patio umbrella eating cake. My father does not prattle on about the state of popular music and my mother is not fussing over a meal she's spent hours cooking. We sit and enjoy the setting sun. Fall leaves drop colors into the grass.

If I were a different daughter, this is where my story would get dark. I would tell you that zombies and witches do exist. That my father is a zombie and I pray that he was turned this way by my mom. That I watched the whole process happen, watched his skin go ashen and his expression turn blank as a plum. That it happened as he ate her poisoned cake and talked about his future. His pulse was slowing as he spoke, but we did not notice. We only realized the change in him when he failed to respond to our simple questions.

This is the moment my father disappeared. Medics came and revived him, but he would never return to his former self. He now shuffles when he walks, and he drools. He needs help getting dressed and wiping his ass. Like a zombie, he does what he is told to do. This is what he feared, but it's also what my father deserves. For the years he controlled everything in our home. For stealing my mother's bright future.

But this is not the story that I will tell because it isn't true. Well, some of it is. But my parents had their understanding. A mother is not the ideas that interest her. Sometimes she's not even her own advice.

It isn't until Day Nine that I have time to call Mike from the hospital. Daddy is tucked beneath sheets and is under the care of a neurologist and a staff of nurses. They think stroke, I tell Mike. They'll run more tests tomorrow. My mother and I are about to have an ugly talk about our health care options.

This will be the second difficult conversation I will have had in a single month. Weeks before, in an office that looked out at Mt. Rainier, my doctor ran down my choices. She said that if I choose surgery, I might have one or two years left to dance. What surgery would do, without question, is bankrupt me and Mike. I could have a somewhat normal life with physical therapy and pain medication.

You can't give up dance, Mike said in our apartment that night in front of Leah and Gordon. We were all drunk and sharing a little too much information. Why not? I asked. Maybe I won't dance on Broadway or win awards, but I've taught hundreds of students. And I'll still choreograph.

But you are a dancer, Mike said. His eyes reflected the fear that a fragile covenant had begun to fray. So what, I said. Why can't I make peace with this and just move on? Because, Leah said, it doesn't work like that. Gordon nodded his head in drunken agreement. You can move on, he said, but we're talking you through this so you won't have any regrets.

Of course I know all about regret: she raised me. She is standing now in the driveway on the morning of Day Twelve. I'm leaving for the airport. I need to tend to things where I live, but I'll return soon.

I'll call if there's any change with your father, my mother says. She pauses then, before asking, Have you made a decision about your surgery? Have you talked to Michael? What does he want you to do?

I listen to her talk. She has questions. She has to get them out before I leave. She has questions. She has a lifetime of concerns.

I'm learning to respect the different roles my mother has mastered through the years—partner, student, thinker, expert, friend. I'm remembering the Christmas we spent in Nassau three decades ago. Mother drove me across the island to the primary school that she attended. She told me how proud granny had been when she was selected by the Victoria League to study abroad. That's how she lived in London and how she ended up here. We looked at the tiny classrooms and desks and then visited the farm where she'd grown up on the western shore. Two old houses stood on the property. One of them reminded me of the shed in our backyard, and the other one was large with white columns and faded green shutters. That's where the British planter lived, in the big house, she said. He owned our land. I was fourteen before I learned that the planter was in fact my old man.

Have you decided? my mother asks me again. No, I say, I haven't decided yet.

I place my suitcase into the trunk of the rental car and turn to hug my mom. We linger in the embrace.

Do you think that you could live with yourself? she asks. Can you live with yourself if you don't dance?

American Industrial Physics

Dear Editors,

Attached please find my submission to *Journal of American Industrial Physics* for your special issue on narrative inquiry.

I am Emeritus Professor of Sociology from Wayne State University, but before obtaining my PhD, I worked for years as a veterinary assistant at Ford Motor Company. My submission is about that work. While Organizational Sociology literature includes numerous studies on automotive crash safety testing, there is little qualitative research focused on the veterinarians who cared for the crash test animals. My research indicates there were over 1,000 veterinarians and veterinary assistants used by the automotive industry between 1955 and 1993. The job of these workers was to maintain and dispose of thousands of animals used in crash tests. I have interviewed several vet assistants, including the author of the narrative below.

Thank you for considering my research for publication.

All best,

Dr. Johnetta Green

1976, Ford River Rouge

Garth said that it was important to our research to have primates of all sizes, some that were over a hundred pounds and some that were smaller, around forty pounds or less. Precious was one of our smaller monkeys, part of *AS Study 993-79: Findings of Forward Impact Crashes on Small Unharnessed Children*. She was a long-tailed macaque with watery eyes, a trait that is common to her species but one made worse by an eye infection that she had when she arrived from the Detroit Zoo. For two weeks after her arrival, I placed antibiotic drops into her eyes. I did this four, maybe six times, each day. The darling never fought or even squirmed. Macaques are generally agreeable, but she was so mild of temperament that Garth remarked, "That one there is just precious," a comment that everyone in Automotive Safety (AS) agreed with, and so the name stuck. But on the day that I prepared Precious for her final crash experiment, I couldn't bring myself to call her by that name.

It was early summer and the mosquitoes nipped and hovered. I walked with Precious from AS to the crash course behind Building D. She crouched in her metal cage and ate green grapes.

No matter how mild a test monkey is, you best believe it can turn violent. They can sense danger and when that happens, watch out, all bets are off. Regina Coker—a vet assistant who wore nails that curved like ram's horns and which were painted a splendid shade of magenta—had her finger bit to the knuckle by a chimpanzee that got spooked by her nails. I expected no less from Precious, though she was silent as we walked to the courseway, her eyes focused, like a penitent, on the trees. Michigan summers are explosions of green, and on that day the auto plant's landscape appeared as lush as a rainforest. The plant is situated where the Rouge and Detroit rivers meet and trees grow leafy from the rich soil.

River Rouge is a city within a city. Precious looked around as if she understood its magnificence. She peered through the cage bars at the tractors hauling this and that, and at the gunmetal smoke that plumed upward from Tool and Dye. There were a slew of buildings at River Rouge and they sprawled for miles in each direction. The place had its own farmland and power plant. There was a complete railroad system and a fire department. It was possible to work there for decades, as I did, and never meet someone who had been there just as long.

In fact, I never saw my son Douglas when he worked at Assembly. I'd gotten him that job thinking it would keep him off the streets, away from the crazies. I worked the day shift, arriving as the sky eased its way to lavender. Garth liked me to be there early to feed and bathe the monkeys.

Strange how attached you can become to an animal. Each morning that I arrived, I'd look for Precious. She slept in a huddle with the other macaques. Like humans, they stayed in their clique, grooming each other, play-fighting, and at night sleeping together on the cage floor, their limbs touching and protecting each other. Garth said that I had a calm demeanor that the animals took to. "You got what they call mother wit," he told me.

Truth is I never have been a good mother. The last time I saw Douglas was in 1981 on the night that I put him out. He was on that stuff: all jittery and thin as a switch. He came in the house talking about job interviews and asking to borrow forty dollars to buy a shirt from Hudson's. "Come on Ma help me out," he said, "I won't get the job if you don't help me." He repeated this like an alarm and then grabbed me by my hair.

In my mind, I could see only three options—we could fight, I could call the police, or I could make Douglas leave. My son was a good foot taller than me and I'll admit I feared him a bit. When a woman thinks of fighting a man, she better have a weapon handy—hot grits, like Al Green's ex-wife, or a stove lid like Mrs. Breedlove in that Morrison book. You got to knock a rascal out. I had neither one.

And I could never *cause* my child to go to jail, so that eliminated option two. "Get the hell out," I told Douglas. He stood there staring me full in my face until my top lip started to sweat. "You know what," he said. "What's that?" I asked him. "Fuck this shit," he said. Then he left. Before he was gone, he stopped in my bedroom and rambled about, but I didn't go back there to check on him. I let him search for what he thought he might find.

When Precious and I got to Building D, a new guard stood in front. She had a pretty brown face but her hair was frosted that brassy blond that the young girls liked back then. The Sunflowers is what I called these girls. "You new?" I asked her.

"No ma'am," she said.

"How long you been here?"

"I been here three years but I'm new to this shift." She smiled.

That's what I mean: there were so many people there doing so many different jobs. You couldn't know them all.

I signed the clipboard and let her look at my badge. When she was satisfied we'd met the procedures, she let me into the building for what we, in AS, called The March.

It was a long walk down a linoleum-tiled hallway that ran through the center of the building. At the end, a glass door led to the courseway. I made that walk plenty of times. To tell the truth, I was relieved that activists started protesting what we did, though it wasn't our studies that initially got their attention but an incident where our heaters malfunctioned one winter, heating up to over 100 degrees. When we found the monkeys the next day, they had either perished or were suffering from kidney failure.

That was a tough day. It wasn't a job every person could do.

I understood what we were doing, though, what Garth was trying to accomplish. We were saving people's lives. We used primates in our research because they're just like us. The injuries they got in those crashes were the same injuries we would get. It used to piss me off when Douglas would degrade what I did, like my job didn't help to feed and clothe him when he was young. I did what I did for him. And I did it for science, too.

Still, I never liked thinking about what happened to the monkeys. I always said a quick prayer for an animal as I put the harness into place. The harness had four metal bars that splayed out like an X, and in the middle was a knob that screwed the harness on tight. We'd put test monkeys inside a car three times before the final ride so they could get used to it. In my prayers, I'd ask that their suffering would not be long. I've said the same prayer for Douglas many, many times.

As I approached the courseway, Precious began rattling about in her cage and making a high-pitched noise. *Uh-oh*, I thought, *this one's about to flip out.* "Shush," I told her and handed her a grape. We stepped through the glass door that blazed white from the summer sun. "You need help with this one?" the test manager asked. "Nah, she's a little one," I replied. I opened the cage and hoisted her delicate frame into my arms. Soon as I touched her, she calmed right down. She clutched my shirt in her fists. I gently pulled on her fingers to get her away from me and into the car's interior. Once she was in, she stood upright and was still.

The harness was like a door that swung from left to right. In the past, I'd swing it shut and turn the knob. Precious would always look at me as I twisted and twisted and twisted. It would take me a while to secure it because she was so tiny. That day we did not twist or swing; instead we just entered the car. Tennessee made child car seats mandatory the year after we published our study.

I remember wishing Precious had shown more fight, but in the end that wasn't her nature. She went into the car like she had on other occasions, as if we would see each other again.

Rebel Airplanes

I.

Joyce swatted at the pine dust settling in her hair. She was sanding *The Etta*, a remote-controlled aircraft that would fly fifty miles above sea level. Once there, it would glide to the edges of outer space to record a clear view of the earth. Steve had shown Joyce a YouTube video of a plane with a similar mission that had failed to keep its video connection. "Shoot," Joyce told Steve when she watched the video. "That's my next project. I want one of my planes to travel to outer space and back."

Of course, she and Steve had talked about this mission before her doctor's prognosis. They'd chatted about it at Santa Monica Beach. Steve had spread a green blanket near the wharf where they sat and ate blueberry crumble and drank drugstore champagne. Afterwards, Joyce lay with her head in Steve's lap and watched the video of the plane on his phone. She cupped her hands around the tiny screen. "You're an inspiration," he had said, which could have meant, at the time, that Joyce was a brilliant engineer. That he believed her planes could accomplish any feat. Those same words spoken today would mean something different. "You're an inspiration" would not refer to her career but to how bravely she was confronting terminal cancer.

Joyce unplugged the DeWalt sander from her garage wall. She remembered the day she became interested in remote-controlled flying. She had just divorced Russell after his sixth extramarital affair. It was early spring, and she had been staring through the window of the county building where she worked as a civil engineer. She was supposed to be updating land-use maps, but instead she stood at the window plotting revenge fantasies about her ex. That's when she saw the red and blue drone. It did loops over the municipal lot. "Steve," she'd said, "Check this out. This little aircraft is making the most daring, sharp-angled moves." Steve looked over the desk that they shared in their open office floor plan. He was supposed to be numbering documents, putting numbers into a database, assigning a file number to groups of documents, but instead he was reading ESPN.com. They were one month into their relationship. Steve folded his arms and stared out the window at the tiny plane, now upside down over the grass, now flying right side up. "Expensive hobby," he'd said to Joyce.

Joyce moved closer to the window that day, her nose touching the glass and leaving behind a greasy mark. She saw the group of men operating the planes. She saw their brightly-colored aircraft zipping past the palms. Look at that, Joyce thought. Folks were flying in the middle of the day when she was trapped inside at work.

Days later, she and Steve built her first plane in Steve's backyard down in Lynwood. She'd build all of her planes at night after work or on weekends. It took forever for the spacers on the first plane to set, and they had to run to the store several times to buy more tubes of epoxy.

"Baby, I'm tired of driving for glue. This time can you tell me exactly how much you're going to need?" Steve asked.

Joyce stared at him. He was not the finest man in the world, but he made Joyce butterscotch pancakes each Saturday, and during their lovemaking her body moved in ways that it never had with her ex. This, she concluded, was love. The secret to love was not to have any expectations and to break all the rules you encounter. If the rules were church wedding, handsome husband, and fuck in a bed, these days Joyce Banks did the opposite.

"Alright, she'd said. I'll run to the store. You watch this wing. If it starts to drop, hold it in place until I get back."

The other challenge with her first plane was beveling the nose ring to make it fit. That had taken forever. But when she was done, her plane, which she named *The Koko*, was nothing short of spectacular. It was lavender and gold, five feet long, and had a wingspan of three feet. Joyce started naming all of her planes after badass blues women: *The Koko. The Billie. Ma Rainey.* The plane Joyce wanted to build now would be smaller than *The Koko*, and it would have a weather balloon that would take it to an altitude of 98,000 feet. That's where the balloon would burst. After that point, the engine would keep her aircraft propelled for about half an hour before it would fall back to earth.

"You always tinkering," the voice said, startling Joyce.

It was her neighbor, Kevin, standing in her driveway. The darkness of night framed him from behind as the light of the garage beamed on his face. Kevin, an enlisted Army soldier, wore a red shirt and camouflage pants. He had his thumbs hooked into his waistband and his head was tilted to the side as he watched her build the plane inside of her detached garage.

"It takes a long time to put this together, Kevin. You should come in here and help me," she said.

"Nah," Kevin said. "I just wanted to stop by and say what's up."

"How's your mother?" Joyce asked.

"She's alright. How's Marquise?"

Joyce put down her tools and walked to the driveway. "He's good, Kev," she said. "He had a game last week against Stanford where he scored twenty points and had six assists."

Kevin stared as if lost in some memory. He did that often since he'd returned from his last tour. Kevin and Marquise had grown up together on this street in central L.A. The violence in the area had changed drastically over the years, but the homes had remained the same. The houses were square and immoveable, what Joyce called apocalypse ready. They were

Spanish-style bungalows made with tiled roofs and premium stucco, materials that were too expensive to use in mass home construction nowadays. As boys, Kevin and Marquise ran between these structures, slamming the metal screen doors as they chased each other. That was back when both of their fathers lived with them. Today, only their mothers were here. Kevin would stay in his mother's house until his next combat tour in the spring. Joyce's son, Marquise, was at UC Davis on a basketball scholarship.

"Tell the baller to get at me next time he's here," Kevin said.

"I will."

Kevin looked around her and into the garage. "What's the assignment for this latest plane?"

Joyce put her hands on her hips and inhaled. Deep breaths helped relieve the throbbing across her back. During her last surgery, doctors sawed off one of her lower ribs, which left a nerve exposed.

"I'm taking this one to a state park," Joyce said. "She's 'bout to fly into outer space."

"No shit?"

"No shit, Kev. You wanna come when I send her up?"

"Nah," Kevin said. "Do your thing, Mrs. Banks. You can tell me about it when you come back home."

Weeks later, when the construction of her aircraft was complete, Joyce drove by herself to the edges of Rios de Los Angeles State Park. *The Etta* was rough in a few places—the wings were crooked, for example—but overall Joyce was pleased with the aircraft and with its radio system. She was less pleased with how long it was taking her to climb out of her truck once she parked. Harder still was walking a few yards away. And she shivered uncontrollably. She could never seem to keep herself warm these days.

She eventually made it to a clearing not far from the park river. Joyce stood there until she could control her movements. This required an intense focus, a turning inward and away from the world around her: the trees, the swarm of gnats hovering over the grass. It's not that she couldn't see these things, but that she tried not to think about them. She would only think of quieting her mind and relaxing her body. Soon, she was standing without moving.

Once her nerves settled, she sent up her plane. *The Etta* rose above the park at a steady clip. Joyce watched the aircraft until it faded into the clouds. Then she watched the FPV. This equipment gave her a view of the plane's trajectory as if she were sitting inside. At 98,000 feet, her weather balloon burst as predicted. She clapped her hands together one time. "Yes! That's how we do it!" she said. Then the plane was in the stratosphere continuing its ascent. Joyce followed its location on the viewer and watched the streamed images. Her plane was flying beyond the heights occupied by commercial aircraft. At seventy minutes after takeoff, Joyce looked at the FPV, saw the curve of the earth against a black background, and she cried. The video connection was crystal clear. She'd done it! Joyce watched the video for several seconds and then began guiding her aircraft back to the park.

She had control of the plane until about 60,000 feet. Then the picture and radio signal went dead. "Shit," she said. Her back hurt, so she bent forward to rest her hands on her thighs. Minutes passed where she did nothing, the pain placing her in a stupor where she couldn't move. This is how her doctor said it would end. Dr. Tutihasi, or Doc Tootie, as Joyce called her. There would be pain, but more significantly, there would be fluid that would slowly leak and rise inside her lungs.

"Basically, I'll drown from within?" she'd asked.

"That's not how I would describe it. Not precisely," Doc Tootie had said.

Joyce would not recall how long she stayed there hunched over like a rock gnome. She would only remember that it seemed like an hour had passed, at least, before the pain in her body finally eased. Chronic pain altered time and space in ways that Joyce didn't fully comprehend even though she recognized that moments were stretching as if elastic. When the pain subsided, she tried again to recover her plane, but the signal was still lost. She packed up her equipment and went to the truck.

"I lost the damn plane," she told Steve when she arrived home.

He was standing in the yard with a garden hose. He was watering grass she'd over-fertilized and burned to a crisp that spring. Her lawn looked like she'd planted hay.

He turned off the water and looked at her.

"That's okay, Joyce. The thing is—you got her up there."

"But I didn't bring her back."

"That's okay."

"No, it's not," Joyce said. She went into the house and slammed the door.

Later that night, as Steve slept in the bed next to her, Joyce sat upright going over each step of constructing *The Etta* in her mind. How could her plane just disappear? Where did it go? She thought back to the first person viewer system and the wiring of the video transmitter. What could she have missed or done differently? Maybe it wasn't the transmitter, but the video downlink or the on-screen display. She'd been suspicious of how cheaply the craft store priced the display. She could handle the idea that she'd made a mistake during the construction, but what she couldn't handle sitting there in her dark bedroom in the middle of the goddamn night was that she'd lost the entire airplane. She had no idea of where it had landed and she'd been too exhausted to search for it when she was at the park. Now, she couldn't even inspect the aircraft to figure out what might have gone wrong.

She called Marquise on the phone. His voice was muffled at first. "Ma?" he answered.

"Honey, are you awake?

"Yeah. Everything okay?"

"No, honey, it's not. I lost my plane."

"Huh?"

"Joyce, who are you talking to?" Steve asked. He was blinking his eyes as he tried to pull himself out of sleep.

"I'm talking to Marquise. Honey? Marquise, you still there?"

"Ma, what'd you say?"

Steve pushed himself into a sitting position. "Baby?"

"I said I lost the plane. All that time and money I spent and I don't even know where the damn thing landed. I'm thinking about going back to the park to search for it, but to be honest, I don't know that I even remember where I was and I didn't keep track of things. That's what's upsetting to me. My methods were really sloppy this time—"

"Baby?"

"What, Steve? What?"

In the silence that followed, Joyce became aware that her right boob had sprung from her nightclothes. It, too, stared at Steve as she turned to face him in the bed. At the same moment, she heard Marquise say in hushed tones, "*It's my mom*," which meant he had been lying next to his own beloved when she called. She was interrupting his life. Like that time when he was a teenager. She had been complaining to him about using up all of her expensive lotion. Then one night, she thought she heard someone in the house and she came out of her bedroom and went into the hall. She heard a noise again in Marquise's bedroom and when she opened his door,

she saw how he had been using lotion to rub himself through the night.

"What is it? I'm talking about *The Etta*," she said to Steve.

She knew she was ridiculous. What sane woman wakes people up to discuss a toy drone with her boob hanging out like some sorry flag?

Her disruptive phone call resulted in one good turn of events. Marquise purchased a train ticket home. He rode the Amtrak to visit her that weekend. He spent some time with Kevin next door. Mostly, though, he followed Joyce around the house. He was there as she washed and folded his clothes, as she looked in the bathroom mirror at her thinning hairline. In every room Joyce entered, Marquise soon followed with his chatter. "Then coach said twelve more laps," he'd say to her, or "We beat them by thirty-five points," or "O-Chem is hard as hell, Ma, but I get to retake the test after our next game." Joyce was thrilled by all of his talk. For years, she suspected that Marquise had so little to say because he hated her for divorcing his dad. His father was an actor who was starring, back then, on a popular network series. Joyce was never able to compete with that. Her work required her to photograph highways and to measure the muddy sewers beneath L.A. She worked underground. She might as well have been a mole, or better yet, a hater, as her son's early social media postings had always reminded her. "Can't wait 2 leave my mama house" he had posted when he was in high school. So it was nice to have him return home as a young man who was unafraid to show her affection. He had not done this since he was little Marquise, the boy who would need orthodontia for overlapping teeth, the one who despised brushing his hair.

She turned from folding his bright pink athletic socks to look up at him. He returned her gaze. "How is Auntie Irma doing?" he asked.

"The same. We should go see her while you're in town."

For years, her aunt Irma had been giving folk hell inside a nursing home that was across the street from a noxious oil field.

"Yeah, we should," Marquise said without a hint of sarcasm.

She decided they would visit the nursing home on that Sunday, before Marquise returned upstate. As they walked into Irma's room, a nurse was handing Irma her medication.

"You're being very nice today, Irma, I appreciate that," the nurse said.

"What did you say? I can't hear you, young man," Irma yelled.

The nurse bent over and raised his voice. "I appreciate that you're cooperating today."

"What did you say? I can't hear you."

The nurse laughed and handed Irma a plastic cup which she took. She lifted it to her lips and dropped a large orange pill into her mouth. The nurse handed her a cup of water which she drank. As Joyce watched this interaction from the doorway, she could feel the nerve in her back jump like a live wire.

"What's the matter with your face?" Irma said to her.

"A back spasm."

"Are you alright?"

"I'm fine."

"Don't lie to me."

"I'm not lying," Joyce said. She closed her eyes and took a deep breath.

When the nurse left the room, Irma bent over and spit the pill into the palm of her hand.

"Auntie!" Marquise said bending down to kiss the older woman's cheek. "You know you were supposed to swallow that. You have to take your medicine so you can feel better."

"That won't make me feel better," Irma said, "but this will." She got up and slid her old feet across the linoleum floor until finally, after several long minutes of walking, she stood in the bathroom next to the toilet. She dropped the pill in the water. It made a plunking sound right before she flushed.

Irma laughed as she slid-walked back to her chair. Within seconds of sitting down, she bowed her head and fell asleep.

Joyce went to the window and looked out at the bobbing pump-jacks. She knew that crude oil didn't come easily out of the ground. It took complex machinery with levers, engines, drills, and suction tubes to force the poison out of the earth's rock.

Irma lifted her head and opened her eyes. "Where's the baby?" she asked. "Is he walking yet?"

"The baby's right here, auntie. He's in college now. Third year," Joyce said.

Irma looked up at her nephew. "Well, I do declare," she said.

On the drive home, they stopped at Wong's for carryout. Joyce had forgotten how much Marquise could eat. Back in her kitchen, she watched him start on his second carton of General Tso's chicken.

"You want to talk about the plane?" he asked.

"I'm working it out in my mind," she said.

"You should take a vacation, Ma," he told her. "You and Steve should go somewhere nice."

Joyce watched as her only child spoke to her. He acted as if this was normal in their relationship, as if he was the one who always thought through their lives and made the wise suggestions.

"That ain't a bad idea," Joyce said. She placed her chopsticks down on her plate. "Hand me my tablet and reading glasses," she said, pointing.

As they ate, she searched online to get a feel for how much a vacation might cost.

But that evening, Joyce had second thoughts about leaving the country. Steve and Marquise double-teamed on her as the three of them drank beer and watched a cable sports channel.

"Joyce, you've been saying you want to get away, and imagine how much good it will do for you to be in another country—a totally different landscape. Different language," Steve said.

"No, I get that part," she said, "believe me I do. But the cost. And what if something happens to me while I'm there?"

"What if something happens to you while you're here? And you never see . . . Norway," Marquise said.

"Norway?"

"Or wherever, Ma. You deserve to get away. You've been working your whole life."

"Why don't I go to Norway?" Joyce asked as she stared at her son. When she looked at Steve, he raised his eyebrows in a silly gesture of agreement.

"Oh, fuck you," she said to Steve. She wasn't convinced. "I've been working my whole life?" Joyce mocked Marquise. She sipped her beer. "Don't bury me yet, boys," she said.

II.

Steve and Joyce arrived in Venice, Italy during *acqua alta*. The flooding was so extreme that year, the water reached mid-shin on Joyce and came up past Steve's ankles as they walked through the city. They carried their shoes in their hands.

"Well this is crazy," Joyce complained. "I can't believe people put up with it. Man, what kind of city planning would you call this?"

They were passing the Basilica di Santa Maria della Salute. In addition to carrying his shoes, Steve had their Nikon camera around his neck. He stopped now to take a photo of the building. Joyce looked down at the water where they, along with several other tourists, stood snapping pictures. One woman accidently dropped her cell phone into the stream.

They were standing in a reflection of the cathedral that was cast across the floodwater. Joyce thought how weird it was that they were taking a picture that the sea had already replicated for them. And weirder still, they were standing right in the middle of the church's reflection, disrupting the watery image with their bodies and foreignness. And she felt foreign. She made this clear to Steve as they walked. She was a foreign creature to the sea. In fact, the sea was making her legs itch. And the tide water's constant motion and smell were making her feel sick.

"I need to go back to the hotel," she said.

A flock of seagulls circled and called overhead. It felt like a sign to her, though of what she wasn't sure.

"Let me get a picture of you first. Walk up the cathedral stairs," Steve said.

She sloshed through the water in her bare feet. The cobblestone loosened in the water and she could feel the sharp grit pressing against the soles of her feet. She noticed, too, the difference in her body's equilibrium and in her mood when she was able to walk out of the water onto higher ground, ground that the tide had not yet covered. This is what evolution must have felt like to those fish that figured out how to leap onto the shore.

She stood on a step in front of the cathedral. "Here?" she asked Steve.

"Move a little to the left," he said.

A woman in a straw hat approached Steve. The hat drooped theatrically about her face. "I'll take the picture. You join her and I can get both of you," she said.

As Steve bounded up the stone steps, the birds circled and swooped closer. Joyce stood there and watched. She felt the sun beat on her scalp and she saw how the light broke into dozens of bright points on the water's surface. The glare was almost blinding. "Let's get this over with," she said to Steve as he joined her on the steps. He wrapped himself around her. She moved into his armpit where she felt warm.

"How do you zoom?" the woman yelled at them.

"The silver button!" Steve shouted back.

"Domani l'acqua sarà più alta," a man standing in the water was saying. "Tutto questo sarà sott'acqua. L'acqua sta salendo. I nostri giorni sono contati!"

"What did he say?" Joyce asked a stranger.

"He said, the tide will be higher tomorrow and all of this will be underwater. The water's rising. He said that our days are numbered."

"Oh, I see the button," the woman said. She stood in the water like a lighthouse. Joyce's lips trembled as she tried to steady her smile for the shot. She was having a horrible time.

That afternoon, they had lunch at a waterside bar, but Joyce's mood remained dour.

"I love your hair," the waiter said to Joyce. He was clearly flirting with her but even that didn't change her disposition. "Where are you from?"

"We're from Los Angeles," Steve said.

"Ah! The city of angels," the waiter said looking at Joyce. "Then let me recommend for my friends from Los Angeles, the *garusoli* as antipasto. It's very, very good."

Joyce looked at the menu and then at Steve. "It's sea snails," she said. She wrinkled her nose.

He shrugged. "When in Venice?" he asked.

"Har-har," Joyce replied. "You so witty."

Steve turned to their waiter. "You said it's good?"

"Very good," the waiter replied.

"Alright, bring us garusoli," Steve announced.

When their food arrived, Joyce was less concerned with tasting a slug than she was with the stinging pain from tiny sores around her mouth. They had first appeared two days before. This morning, in the hotel room, she kept turning her head as Steve tried to kiss her on the mouth.

"Kiss me," he'd said, either because he was blind or just so horny he didn't care. But she insisted that he do other things with his mouth and she offered her neck, and clitoris, and toes as substitutes. They ended up having sex while standing. Steve entered her gently from behind, careful not to bend or place too much pressure on her back. At one time, this position made Joyce feel desirable, but this morning it made her feel that she might break.

"To sea snails with my beautiful woman," Steve said. He raised a glass of red wine.

Joyce first noticed her shortness of breath in the gondola. It was the day before they would return home. They were in a canal passing a row of crowded cafes. Joyce felt the tightening in her chest. She felt lightheaded as well. *Aggressive* is how Doc Tootie had described her lung cancer during Joyce's last office visit. But in spite of her onset of breathlessness, Joyce felt oddly at ease. Maybe it was the rocking of the boat or the wind. Or the sight of so many attractive people sitting at tables outside of cafes. Whatever the cause, Joyce felt like she had adapted, momentarily, to her watery surroundings. The irony was, after days of feeling uneasy, it was time for her to return home.

That's how her timing had always been in life. For example, once she'd gotten used to marriage, that shit fell apart.

"I'm thinking of filing for divorce," Joyce had told her auntie Irma years ago, before they both fell sick. It had taken her a while to get it, but Joyce finally understood that her marriage was done. Without missing one beat, Irma suggested that they hold a wake.

"Why not?" Irma said, "and I'm not talking sad or Pentecostal. Think New Orleans–style funeral. I'll bring some Hennessy."

They chose a weekend when Russell was in the valley filming a pilot episode. The ceremony, "Free at Last: A Farewell to Russell in Three Acts," took place in Joyce's living room. They placed programs on dining room chairs that they had lined into neat rows. On the cover of the program were awkward photos of Joyce and Russell throughout the years, their expressions ones of boredom or hunger, except for one photo taken in Puerto Vallarta. In that photo, they smiled. On it, Irma drew curled bison horns over Russell's head.

"To spare us from having to look at this tragedy," Irma said, "this marriage has requested a closed casket."

Joyce disrupted her auntie's speech with drunken laughter. "I thought we said my marriage would be cremated."

"Or annulled," Irma said, "let's have your marriage annulled." She turned to face the empty chairs. "This shit never happened, people. Thank you for coming. End of service."

Oh, how clever they had felt. How clever and how pissy drunk.

What a different perspective Joyce had about it all today. Those years with Russell were just a blip, and had not been worth the time she'd spent grieving. She stared now at the masonry on the bridge as her gondola approached it. This was the oldest bridge in Venice, the gondolier was telling them. Built in 1181.

"Made out of stone?" she asked.

"No, the first bridge was wooden," the gondolier said. "It received fire damage in the revolt in 1310. And then it collapsed from the weight of crowds in 1444 and 1524. Then when we rebuilt it, we made it strong with stone."

Her breathing became shallow and more labored on their flight home.

"I think I know what went wrong with The Etta," she said to Steve between quick breaths.

"Save your breath, you can tell me later."

"I'm fine," she said. She took a sip of her airplane water.

"Did you call Doc Tootie to make an appointment?" he asked.

Joyce nodded. "I see her on Wednesday afternoon."

She continued. "I think next time I'm going to use something that pulls the space tighter in the cavity that holds the battery. There was a gap there. That could have caused the deans connectors to disengage from the power source. And I'm going to put a GPS tracker on my plane the next time," she said.

"Sounds like a plan," Steve replied.

Sixteen hours after they boarded a plane at Marco Polo Airport, they pulled up to Joyce's house in central L.A. Everything was as she'd left it. The houseplants were wilted, but still alive. The mail, mostly bills, had accumulated in the mailbox on her front porch. Seeing the bills reminded Joyce that she needed to make a payment to her doctor and to check on her sick leave from work.

Her garage was in remarkable disarray. She'd never straightened up from her last plane. She stepped around a cardboard box to look at her aircraft. Three out of the four planes she'd built over the years were sitting there on the garage floor.

Kevin walked up her driveway as she stood out there looking at her work.

"Welcome back," he said.

"Thanks, Kev."

"I know you just got in and everything, but I wanted to be the first one to say hello."

"I appreciate that."

He looked at her messy garage-turned-hangar.

"Let me know when you get back in here. Maybe I can help before I go overseas," he said.

"It's a deal, Kev. I'm tired right now, but probably in a day or so I'll be out here at night and I'll come get you. Okay?"

"Cool," he said.

"Kevin," Steve said, "could you help me carry Joyce's bags inside?"

Steve and Kevin carried her luggage in the house and then Steve moved back toward the door.

"I'm just gonna show Kevin out," he said to her.

"Go ahead," Joyce replied.

She couldn't believe how much energy Steve had when she was feeling so depleted. And hot. Her body burned as if on fire. She went to her bedroom and struggled into her nightclothes. Through the closed window, she could hear Steve's laughter as he talked with Kevin. They were discussing remote-controlled aircraft. Soon, she heard them dragging her work table across the garage floor. Then she heard the scrape of metal and the slap of wooden planks.

She turned on the television and climbed slowly into her bed. A while later, Steve walked into the room.

"You feeling okay?" he asked.

The fever hummed inside her ears. "I'm alright," Joyce said.

She lay in her bed, her chest rising and falling in a rapid motion. She watched the newscasters talk their silly news jargon. Why did they all enunciate the exact same way?

Steve sat on the bed next to her. He lifted her head and placed it on his lap. He smoothed his hand over her tight curls.

"What were you and Kevin doing?" she asked.

"We were cleaning up the garage so you can get back in there."

"You mean *if* I get back in," she said. She closed her eyes and breathed through her mouth.

"You will," Steve said in a small voice.

"Oh, I know," she lied.

As she drifted off, she thought about the fact that Steve could discover, hours from now, that she no longer cleaved to the body in bed beside him. She hoped that discovery would not destroy him. She hoped he would remember that impermanence was essential to their work. The materials and then construction. Then the weather. Then time.

How to Leave the Midwest

for Deletha Word*

It must be, DeAnn thought, that her sister was not a sexy thirteen. Not like DeAnn had been the year before. She gathered this by the way the boys in gold chains paused to look up and down at Crystal, and then turned hugely away. DeAnn had warned Crystal about her little girl hairdos. That day, her sister wore her hair in an Afro puff, which sat like a geranium on the crown of her head. "Not cute," DeAnn had told her. Crystal said that DeAnn's straightened flip, which swept down over one of DeAnn's eyes, made her look, quote, extra cheap.

DeAnn was not insulted—was never insulted—by Crystal's assessment of her, especially when the boys in chains were turning to glance at DeAnn

---

* On August 19, 1995, 33-year-old Deletha Word fell to her death from the Belle Isle Bridge into the Detroit River. Ms. Word died following a violent confrontation on that bridge with Martell Welch, Jr., wherein Welch beat her and tore off her clothing in front of dozens of witnesses, following a minor auto accident. Afraid for her life, Word, who could not swim, tried to escape by leaping into the water.

again. DeAnn was cute. Boys liked her because she was cute. Boys wanted to have sex with her. She liked sex. She'd had sex at least a dozen times, maybe two dozen times. These encounters happened in basements, swimming pools, in wooded fields, at the mall, or in cars if the boys could drive. She couldn't explain how incredible it felt to be with a boy in an unlikely place, then return home to eat dinner with her mother and sister. It felt the way Christmas felt before you knew. It felt like someone out there thought you were special. Sometimes, before she did it, DeAnn thought she might explode into a cloud of atoms from anticipation. But afterward, as she'd pull on her jeans, she never felt special. She felt nothing. Mostly, she felt alone.

If she had to live here—in a city that offered her nothing and with parents who moved her toward new terrors—she would, at least, try for sexy.

The boys were still checking her out when DeAnn looked over at them. They stood near the school staircase, a huddle of backpacks, chains, sneakers. DeAnn and Crystal had not gone to public school in years, since Crystal was in second grade and DeAnn in third, so when they walked through the doors of Edward Bigley High School that morning, DeAnn was holding her breath, trying to feel how her body was different from the jangle of sounds and rhythms she would join. It was her father's idea that the girls attend a regular high school.

"Where's your homeroom?" DeAnn asked.

Crystal unfolded her class schedule and examined it. "Mr. Glover. Third floor," she said.

They looked up at the same time. Bigley High was enormous, so big it had elevators. Her mom said that when she'd gone there, the post–World War II boom had swelled the graduating classes to close to a thousand teenagers. In the late sixties, a separate L-shaped wing had been attached to the original building to accommodate the sudden surge in students. Now, there were half that many kids in the whole school, and the emptiness made the smallest sound echo throughout the eight floors. From the outside the school looked like a big warehouse, like everything else in Detroit.

"I'll meet you at this staircase at the end of the day," DeAnn told Crystal.

"We have the interview," Crystal said.

"I know."

She watched her younger sister navigate past a group of big-bodied girls. Crystal moved ungracefully: she did a duck-walk down the wide hall.

DeAnn started toward her first class. From her peripheral vision, she saw one of the boys break from the group and begin following her. She stopped to tie her shoe.

"What's up, you new?" the boy asked.

She stayed crouched on the floor and peered up at him with her one exposed eye.

There were no boys at her previous school, Our Lady of Mercy College Preparatory Academy. DeAnn chose her boyfriends back then from the sons of judges, doctors, and legislators with whom her parents socialized. These were preppy boys who, like DeAnn, lived in neighborhoods of the city where grand homes overlooked tennis courts and a golf course. These boys bought her designer purses in exchange for the blow jobs that she gave them.

"Who's your homeroom teacher?" the boy asked.

"The name sounds like icky?"

"Miss Nozicki."

"That's it," DeAnn said.

The boy had the whitest sneakers she'd ever seen, and a chipped tooth that was graying. Probably from a fight, De Ann thought.

"Miss Nozicki never takes attendance. You can ditch her class."

DeAnn looked to her left and then right. "Where would I go if I ditched? There isn't much around here."

"I drove. We could hang out at Belle Isle," he said. He ran his fingers over the leather face of her purse. "Nice," he said. "The new Guccis got dope design."

"Thanks," DeAnn said.

"So, you coming?"

"Maybe. Are you a senior?"

"Not exactly," the boy said.

They left campus through a remote door in the B-wing. DeAnn felt the usual thrill; it rattled in her shins as she walked. She had high expectations for their day. Her father believed in high expectations, not for skipping school, but in professional life. That's why he was not content to be a judge and wanted to run for Congress. That's why her dad had formed a political action committee, and why their family would sit for an interview this afternoon with Channel Four News. At one time, DeAnn thought, her family at least pretended to be about academics. It was the reason she and Crystal had attended Our Lady of Mercy. In his conversations with other adults, her father had often mentioned the value of a good education, and the "fight that King waged for little black girls and boys." Now, DeAnn and Crystal were attending Bigley, which was a decent high school, though nothing extraordinary. DeAnn's dad said they were going to Bigley to save money for college. DeAnn understood something different. Her father would have more in common with voters if his daughters attended a public school. But he couldn't say that, just like DeAnn couldn't say that she liked sex. True desires, DeAnn knew, were best kept folded inside your pocket.

She climbed into the boy's car, which was expensive and smelled of the vanilla air freshener they sell at the car wash. He lit a joint and they smoked. Outside the window, the struggling businesses on Jefferson Avenue rolled past like a scene from a detective show. Soon she saw the glittering top of the river as the car drove onto the bridge that led to the municipal island. She was not supposed to be on the island; it was dangerous. In the late nineties, a woman had been beaten on the Belle Isle bridge until she jumped to her death into the river. But that was years ago and DeAnn believed she could protect herself.

The boy parked in the middle of the island next to the water. DeAnn noticed, on the other side of the river, the sad, boxed-shaped buildings of Windsor, Canada, and she thought of her mother. That morning before leaving for school, she saw the keloidal scar where her mothers' breasts used to be. DeAnn pulled off her T-shirt. "Your tits are big," the boy told her, "bigger than the rest of your body." DeAnn ignored this. She slid her tongue beneath the rough edge of his chipped tooth. She climbed on top of him and unzipped his jeans. She rocked back and forth and watched his head fall back on the leather headrest as he came. She liked watching him let go.

When they were done, he rolled down the windows and wiped his sweaty forehead with the edge of his shirt. "I'm thirsty," he said. "You want to go to my place and get a bottle of water?"

"Will your parents be at home?" De Ann asked. Her mother did not work. Not before the surgery or after.

"I have my own place not far from here."

She looked at his leather car seats and gold necklace. "Are you a drug dealer?" she asked.

He laughed. "Bitch, stop asking me questions before I have to kill you."

DeAnn believed this was one of those jokes that could reveal if she were cool or a punk. She decided not to act unnerved.

He drove to Van Buren Avenue just on the outskirts of downtown. The buildings on Van Buren were more rundown than those on Jefferson had been. At least Jefferson Avenue had the mirrored General Motors building and a view of the river. Here, in the middle of the city where everything was concrete and gray, the storefronts had hand-painted signs and bars over the windows. There was no pretense of urban revitalization in this neighborhood.

They pulled up to a dark building that had a Mohawk Vodka ad painted onto its brick façade. Now it was DeAnn's turn to be sarcastic. "Oh nice," she said. "You live in an abandoned building?"

"It ain't abandoned. It just looks that way," he said.

He told her his name was Curtis and led her through a side door. DeAnn noticed that there wasn't a proper lobby and that the floor was concrete that had not been covered with carpeting or tiles. DeAnn saw a few doors but they lacked apartment numbers.

"We have to go up to the second floor," he told her. He approached an elevator shaft where a freight car should have been. There was no door over the shaft. Instead there was just a huge canyon that looked like it could swallow you whole. DeAnn was no longer amused.

"How old are you?"

"I'm twenty. I graduated from Bigley two years ago."

He pushed the button to call the elevator car. He turned to look at DeAnn. She'd stopped several feet away.

"The building's raw, I know," he said. "A handful of artists live here. You have to hear about the place from someone who knows." As he talked, the freight elevator appeared before them.

"We can take the stairs if you'd feel more comfortable."

"You're an artist?" DeAnn asked. "Art student," he said. "I'm studying industrial design."

Curtis unlocked the door to his loft, which was one long sweep of workman space. The unit was big enough to fit a table saw, lathe, and other woodcutting equipment. A wooden wardrobe that he'd made sat in the middle of the room. There were no straight lines on the wardrobe, only wavy ones, its legs as curvy as a woman's. The furniture looked alive. It looked like something drawn by Dr. Seuss.

"That's different," DeAnn said.

"One of my professors wants to enter it into an exhibition in New York," Curtis said. He ran his hand along the left side of the wardrobe.

"How did you know you could do this?" she asked.

"Do what? Make furniture?"

"Yeah."

"I didn't."

Curtis walked over to a compact refrigerator and retrieved two bottles of water. "I better call the school," DeAnn remembered. She dialed the school office on her cell phone. "Hi, this is Judge Porter's wife," she began. "I'm calling to let you know that my daughter came home this morning. She wasn't feeling well. DeAnn Porter. Thank you."

Curtis looked at DeAnn. DeAnn looked at the loft. Clearly, it had not been renovated for residential use. Wires sprouted from some of the electrical sockets. The floors were unfinished. The room lacked insulation and was cold.

DeAnn decided that she could never live in this building, but being there made her believe that she could live somewhere else. Somewhere unexpected.

Curtis walked over to her with the water. When she'd taken a sip and had placed the bottle on the floor, he took her hand and placed it on his cock. She gently squeezed his testicles. She wondered if she'd ever get used to how male genitals felt and looked. Testicles reminded her of jellied sea creatures.

"What's so funny?" he asked.

"Nothing," she said. To stifle her laughter, she practiced a sultry look. She narrowed her eyes and slowly parted her lips.

Curtis dropped her off at school before the end of seventh period. She entered the school through the same door through which she'd left. She passed the rows of empty classrooms in the B-Wing. Why were so many buildings empty in the city?

Soon the bell rang and DeAnn was in a section of the school where kids ran about the hallways talking smack. She made her way to the staircase. She saw Crystal's profile from among the crowd. From that angle, DeAnn saw how her sister's upswept hair complimented her long, slender neck. Two boys walked past Crystal and looked her over. "Erykah Badu," one of them said. "Erykah Ba-doo-doo," the other one cracked. DeAnn elbowed past them.

"Where have you been?" Crystal asked her.

"Come on," DeAnn said, "I saw mom's car out front."

Their mother sat in a Volvo at the curb. She looked relieved to see their faces. "How was your first day?" she asked as they climbed inside. "Bigley's not bad, huh?" DeAnn saw that it had not been a good day for her mother. Her mom had dark circles beneath her eyes. DeAnn hated pretending that her mom's life was not collapsing around her knees. "It was perfect," DeAnn replied.

They arrived home as the Channel Four News truck drove up their tree-lined street and onto their circular driveway. DeAnn's mother pulled the car into the garage. Her father met them there in a pale blue shirt and red tie.

He looked at his watch.

"That was a little close," he said to DeAnn's mother.

When DeAnn got out of the car, she saw her father's eyes move over her body with the proprietary look that she hated. "Precious, go comb your hair out of your eyes," he said.

DeAnn went to the bathroom off the foyer. She left the door open and watched as her sister and mother went to greet the news people, who were now coming through their front door with lights and cameras. DeAnn grabbed a comb from the drawer within the vanity. She pulled it through her thick roots. She knew that she stood inside her house although she felt anywhere but there. She was outside the bathroom window, above the Mohawk Vodka building. She was igniting far away: exploding, emerging, gone.

She decided her hair was fine and joined her family on the sofa. When the photographer began his urgent clicking, she stared down the camera's dark lens.

Meet Behind Mars

Dear Dr. Lutz,

You've requested that I write a statement to the school board about The Night of the Yellow Mustard Penis, and I've tried to pull together all of the evidence that I have. In the process, I've remembered other incidents that have happened over the years, like The Bullying with a Dead Leaf Incident, or The Case of Sexual Harassment with Gummy Worms. The worm incident happened when Jesse was just in second grade. Recalling this has been hard for me, Dr. Lutz, and I feel like I can't tell one story about a giant mustard penis because it's not about a mustard penis only, but about all of these incidents together, in context, and through time. It's also about education and the fact that I'm a black woman who lives alone with her son. It's about lots of stuff, some of which I tried to include in this statement but most which I decided to leave out. The worst part of writing this statement was recalling all of these events because, honestly, I'd just as soon forget. Anyway, I'm including email and voicemail messages along with my written thoughts. I hope this is acceptable to your board members.

Sincerely,

Jesse's Mom

Gloria Clark

FROM: Rachel Manning <manning@dusd.edu>
TO: Gloria Clark <gc66@gmail.com>
DATE: October 2011

Good Afternoon, Ms. Clark,

Jesse bullied another student today by placing a leaf on the boy's shirt. He told the boy that the leaf was a bug and Jesse knows that this student is scared of bugs. I thought that you should know.

Sincerely,

Rachel Manning

TO: Rachel Manning <manning@dusd.edu>
FROM: Gloria Clark <gc66@gmail.com>
DATE: October 2011

Hi Mrs. Manning,

I'm confused. Is this child blind?

Sincerely,

Jesse's mom

TRANSCRIBED VOICEMAIL MESSAGE

April 2009

Hi, Gloria, this is Adrienne Kuchanick, principal at Middleton Elementary. I wanted you to know that I gave Jesse two after-school detentions for bringing a weapon to school. Yeah . . . (PAUSE) . . . he was found in possession of a nail file at recess. Now, usually the consequences for this are suspension or expulsion. Bringing a weapon to school is a big No-No that we take very seriously within our district. But I showed Jesse some leniency by giving him after-school detentions because he's a good kid. And he's such a cutie!! But he cannot bring weapons to school. Let me know if you have any questions. Okay. Thanks, Gloria. Bye-bye.

FROM: Gloria Clark <gc66@gmail.com>
TO: Adrienne Kuchanik <akuchanick@dusd.edu>
DATE: April 2009

Dear Principal Kuchanick,

This may be too much information but we don't own any nail files in our home.

Sincerely,

Jesse's mom

TRANSCRIBED VOICEMAIL MESSAGE

April 2009

Hi Gloria,

Principal Kuchanick, here. I received your email. After further investigation, we discovered that another boy brought the nail file to school. But Jesse was the one holding the file when the recess teacher found it. Apparently a bunch of boys were standing around and playing with this very sharp tool. All of the boys are serving after-school detentions. Thanks for your support of our rules. Let me know if you have further concerns. Okay. Take care. Bye-bye.

FROM: Elena Guitierrez <guitierrez@dusd.edu>
TO: Gloria Clark <gc66@gmail.com>
DATE: September 2008

Hello,

I wanted you to know that I had to speak to Jesse about sexual harassment today. I caught him and a few other boys placing gummy worms near their privates and laughing with each other in class. There were girls in the class who saw this lewd display. I talked to Jesse about appropriate and inappropriate behavior with gummy worms.

Let me know if you have questions.

Elena Guitierrez

Lead Second Grade Teacher

FROM: Adrianne Kuchanick <akuchanick@dusd.edu>
TO: Gloria Clark <gc66@gmail.com>
DATE: November 2012

Hi Gloria,

I wanted to let you know that we got a call from a parent who saw Jesse looking at graffiti on one of the foreclosed homes in the neighborhood. Please remind him that this is private property and to walk straight home from school.

Sincerely,

Principal Kuchanick

FROM: Gloria Clark <gc66@gmail.com>
TO: Brian Carlson <bcarlson@dusd.edu>
DATE: October 2013

Dear Mr. Carlson,

When I checked Gradebook I saw that Jesse has zeros for assignments when he was out of town. I sent you emails before he traveled to make sure he could make up those assignments. Did you get those emails? Thanks for helping me keep him on track.

Best, Gloria

FROM: Gloria Clark <gc66@gmail.com>
TO: Brian Carlson <bcarlson@dusd.edu>
DATE: October 2013

Hi Mr. Carlson,

You have Jesse marked as absent in Gradebook on days that he was excused to travel to Oakland to visit his dad. I apologize if you didn't get my messages. I'm thinking my emails went into your spam.

Sincerely,

Jesse's Mom

FROM: Gloria Clark <gc66@gmail.com>
TO: Brian Carlson <bcarlson@dusd.edu>
DATE: November 2013

Mr. Carlson,

Jesse insists that he turned in the Algebra assignments marked as missing in Gradebook. I am trying to keep him accountable. Did you get those assignments from him?

Jesse's Mom

FROM: Brian Carlson <bcarlson@dusd.edu>
TO: Gloria Clark <gc66@gmail.com>
DATE: January 2014

Hey Gloria,

Jesse knows that he's not doing all of his work. He's not being honest with you. I understand that his dad is not around and it's probably hard for you to keep up with everything as a single parent. I've told Jesse, look, your mom has moved you to a good school district, got you in advanced math, and you need to take advantage of this opportunity and not mess it up. Bottom line is Jesse needs to work a little harder.

Yours,

Brian

In addition, Dr. Lutz, I'd like to include the advertisement for the home that attracted me to your school district:

Desirable Durant, WA rambler! Open and inviting floor plan. Large kitchen with hickory cabinets and Pergo flooring. Spacious living room with cozy brick fireplace. Newer exterior paint. Big fenced back yard. Views of Olympic Mountains and Sequalitchew Creek. Located in great neighborhood. RV parking. Good Schools! Walking distance to Middleton Elementary.

You see, Mr. Carlson is right that I was interested in Durant because of its schools. He's also right that I am single, which is announced on the deed to the house that I own:

Statutory Warranty Deed

∞

Grantor(s): Stacey Flanahan and John Flanahan, wife and husband

Grantee(s): Gloria V. Clark, an unmarried woman

But the fact that I'm a single mother who moved to a decent school district is no big deal, right? I mean, people do that every day. So why did Mr. Carlson feel the need to bring it up? And why did I feel dirty as I read his response? It reminded me of what Thurgood Marshall said in his closing arguments in *Brown v. Board of Education*. I know this argument by heart because Jesse memorized it when he portrayed Thurgood Marshall at History Night in the 6th grade. In his closing remarks, Marshall said, and I quote,

"So whichever way it is done, the only way that this Court can decide this case in opposition to our position (of school desegregation), is that there must be some reason which gives the state the right to make a classification that they can make in regard to nothing else in regard to Negroes, and we submit the only way to arrive at that decision is to find that for some reason Negroes are inferior to all other human beings."*

Those last eight words get at what I'm trying to say to you, Dr. Lutz. That's what's underneath Mr. Carlson's email and all of these messages. These messages show what members of this school community really think of me and Jesse when they look at us. They think that we'll stab them with a Revlon

---

* *Brown v. Board of Education of Topeka*, 347 U.S. 483 (1954). This excerpt of Thurgood Marshall's closing argument in the *Brown* case is taken from *Ripples of Hope: Great American Civil Rights Speeches* (New York: Basic Civitas Books, 2003).

nail file. They think it's fascinating that we live in this neighborhood. They think of nooky. Take this discussion I had with another mom at family orientation when Jesse was in the first grade:

> PARENT: "Hi, I'm Michelle."
> ME: "Hi, I'm Gloria"
> MICHELLE: "Which child is yours?"
> ME: "Um, the black boy in the class."
> MICHELLE: "You mean Jesse! My Becca talks about Jesse all of the time."
> ME: "Okay" (confused because I'd never heard of Becca before).
> MICHELLE: "I think they have crushes on each other."
> ME: "Really?"
> MICHELLE: "Oh, yeah. Becca thinks Jesse is cute. Becca talks about him all of the time."
> ME: (Head down. Furiously searching for something in my purse.)

Or this exchange with Jesse's kindergarten teacher when I was volunteering in the classroom one day:

> TEACHER: Jesse is a real leader in this class.
> ME: That's great! We—
> TEACHER: You can tell that he will be the life of the party when he's older. He and his buddy, Vershawn, are going to be so popular. They're so cute. They almost look like brothers.

When I remember these incidents, Dr. Lutz, I recall what my sister said when I told her that I was moving to Durant, Washington. "Why you moving out to Mars?" she asked. "There aren't a lot of people who look like us out there." And I defended this place to my sister. I didn't tell her that Durant wasn't Mars, because most days it feels like a foreign planet. But I told her that I had a right to sail across the universe if I wanted, and to meet behind Mars with my beloveds like Cheryl Lynn sang in 1978, when we were twelve and fourteen years old and listening to her song on our mother's car radio. We'd be curled up like roly-polies in the backseat, singing, and our mother would be in the driver's seat surrounded by light streaming through the windshield and the smoke from her cigarette. Back then, my sister probably imagined "making star love" to one of her boyfriends, but when I listened to "Star Love," I heard a call to go wherever I damn pleased, and to expect good things when I showed up.

Anyway, this is how I answered Mr. Carlson:

FROM: Gloria Clark <gc66@gmail.com>
TO: Brian Carlson <bcarlson@dusd.edu>
DATE: January 2014

Dear Mr. Carlson,
Can we arrange for a time to meet? I just got Jesse's state testing and he's in the 94th percentile in math but he has a C in your class. I'm trying to understand this discrepancy. Thanks. Gloria Clark.

I never heard back from Mr. Carlson. I went to the assistant principal. I told him about Gradebook, the test scores, how I'd seen Mr. Carlson talking to people in the parking lot during school hours. How Mr. Carlson was absent every week. How he refused to communicate with me. The assistant principal said he would have Mr. Carlson get in touch with me, but Carlson never did. Then the following year, Jesse was placed in Algebra 1-2 again, despite the fact that we'd registered for the next course, Algebra 3-4. And when I asked the principal why Jesse was taken off the fast track, she said Mr. Carlson recommended it and she would talk to him because she wasn't sure why he made this decision, looking at Jesse's test scores and grades. Well, Mr. Carlson never responded to her, and so she placed Jesse back in 3-4. Then a few weeks later, we learned that Mr. Carlson had been arrested for dealing and using drugs on the school campus.

Jesse is fifteen years old now. Here is correspondence I've received from his teachers about him this year:

"Jesse is receiving a lunch detention for failure to keep his hands to himself. We have zero tolerance for touching in the hallways. Jesse hugged another student. This was caught on camera."

"Jesse is receiving a lunch detention for wearing his jeans too low. When he bends over at his locker, cameras show his gym shorts sticking out from beneath his jeans."

"Jesse is receiving a lunch detention for activity seen on hall cameras. He and another student were jumping up trying to touch the top of the lockers."

"Jesse is laughing too much in Spanish. Spanish is not a funny class."

"Jesse takes too long to tie his shoes in the locker room and is late coming out for class."

And then there is the incident involving kids from his high school, which prompted this statement that I write to you:

FROM: Gloria Clark <gc66@gmail.com>
TO: Officer Nesbitt <fxnesbitt@dusd.edu>
DATE: February 2015

Dear School Officer Nesbitt,
Could you please come investigate a yellow mustard penis drawn on my driveway? I believe the picture was drawn by girls at the high school.

FROM: Officer Nesbitt <fxnesbitt@dusd.edu>
TO: Gloria Clark <gc66@gmail.com>
DATE: February 2015

Dear Ms. Clark,
Tell me more about the mustard penis. Do you have pictures of it?

TO: Officer Nesbitt <fxnesbitt@dusd.edu>
FROM: Gloria Clark <gc66@gmail.com>
DATE: February 2015

Officer Nesbitt,

Here are pictures of the mustard penis. And here are pictures of the message "fuck y" that was drawn on my garage door. (I assume the girls ran out of mustard to draw the letters o and u). Also please find pictures of a busted watermelon and Kool Aid Jammers that were thrown at the house. The perpetrators are 9th grade white girls who did this at midnight. My son was having a birthday sleepover at the time. Jesse's guests were 9th grade black boys who also go to the school. As punishment, I would like these girls to stand in front of the watermelon and mustard penis and perform an interpretive dance.

TO: Gloria Clark <gc66@gmail.com>
FROM: Officer Nesbitt <fxnesbitt@dusd.edu>
DATE: February 2015

Ms. Clark,

I have looked at the photos and contacted parents. We cannot ask the girls to perform a dance, but they have written letters of apology, which I'm attaching below.

> Dear Mrs. Clark,
> I'm so sorry for what we did to you and your house. It will never ever happen again. There was no intent to be racist towards anyone and I'm sorry if you felt that way.
>
> Sincerely, Miley

> Dear Mrs. Clark,
> I would like to formally apologize for pranking your property. It was out of childish humor and ended up turning into something worse. This will never happen again and I hope you forgive my friends and I.
>
> From, Sarah

Gloria,

I'm sorry for doing that to your house. The reasons we used watermelon is because one of the boys asked for it on their Snapchat story. The Kool-Aid was just something to drink.

Sincerely,

Christi

Christi's response (that the girls only came to my home bearing gifts) reminds me of one last thing that I want to say, Dr. Lutz.

I can't really do much with the girls' letters of apology except put them in this statement to the school board. I wish the girls had done an interpretive dance instead. They could have used streamed music or live instruments. They could have put those awful-sounding wind recorders from fourth grade to good use. They could have designed costumes: long skirts with bells, or leggings and sparkly T-shirts purchased from Justice and Pink. They could have danced with or without shoes. That alone is something. Only brave souls step in bare feet on the cold moss and rocks. They would have had to move around and through each item thrown against my house. The red melon that peeked through its cracked shell. The shiny mass-produced Jammers that won't decay, that will end up floating somewhere with other junk in the Pacific. It would have been interesting to see whether they stepped on the yellow balls drawn from their imaginations, whether they absorbed the color and substance into their own skin or performed around it in deference to or fear of the image and idea. Would they have danced in the sun? Or come again at night? There would have been so many decisions for them to make! See, a letter leaves the work to me to translate what they really think. But a dance! Now a dance would have shown me who those girls are.

I don't feel that type of revealing between *neighbors* is too much to ask, do you Dr. Lutz? I patiently await your response.

Sincerely,

Gloria Clark